THE BOOK OF SECRETS

THE LAST ORACLE BOOK ONE

MELISSA MCSHANE

Night Harbor Publishing

ISBN-13 9781949663204

Cover design by Alexandra Brandt http://www.alexandrajbrandt.com

Cover images © Gutaper | Dreamstime.com

© Ylivdesign | Dreamstime.com

Dedicated to all the owners of tiny, hidden-away bookstores everywhere, whose powers of finding just the right book are truly magical

1

Bookstores were supposed to smell of old leather and dry paper. This one smelled of onion, of musty dry air trapped for centuries underground, smells that hung in the frigid air like invisible curtains. Aside from my own breath, the store was perfectly still, without even the *whoosh* of passing traffic to remind me of the world outside.

I took a few steps toward the bookcases, peering around them for some sign of Mr. Briggs. Should I wait for him, or did he expect me to follow while he answered the phone? I'd had exactly three job interviews in my life, not counting the one that had gotten me the job at McDonald's the summer I was sixteen, and I had no idea what the protocol was. My shoes, sensible pumps, tapped quietly across the cracked yellow linoleum, spangled with silver stars that time had worn to gray blisters. Still no sign of life.

I straightened my skirt and took a seat on the folding chair next to the door. I stifled a shriek when my bare legs brushed the freezing metal. The chair wobbled when I shifted my weight, and I held still, afraid it might dump me off. I really didn't want to touch the floor. It wobbled again, and I shot to my feet. Maybe standing was the better option.

The wooden counter to my left was curved plywood stained walnut-dark, topped with a sheet of glass cracked like the linoleum. A stack of remaindered pop psychology books declaring I could Master My Potential! weighed it down at one end, and the antique cash register took up the other. It looked more like an art piece than anything functional, with brass filigree decorating its sides and back, and a Victorian valentine complete with lace appliqued to the top. It was hard to believe it was anything more than a conversation piece, but I'd seen Mr. Briggs use it when handling a sale ten minutes ago, so it wasn't a joke.

It had been a surprise when someone actually bought a book. I didn't think anyone was brave enough to squeeze between the shelves. They were packed so tightly that if two people tried to negotiate the same aisle, one would have to back up to let the other pass. The highest shelves were well beyond the reach of an ordinary person, at least eight feet tall, and I hadn't seen a stepladder. And the books... it made me shudder to look at them, crammed in any old way, flat on their faces or standing at attention, with more books piled on the tops of the bookcases. The idea of this going on for several hundred square feet gave me chills.

I went to the nearest bookcase and examined the titles. There was no theme to their organization: a cookbook sat next to a book on the Prussian military campaign in 1805, which was next to a novel titled *Translations in Celadon*. I removed a book and sniffed its spine. It smelled just as it ought, of dry paper and dust, and that reassured me. The store might be strange, the organization nonexistent, but at least the books were sound. I'd half-expected to smell mildew or cigarette smoke.

I heard a distant voice, barely more than a whisper. "Hello?" I said. "Mr. Briggs?" The whispering stopped. A draft of frigid air brushed my ear, making goose pimples rise up on my arms. The voice spoke again, but I still couldn't understand it. I turned around fast, suddenly nervous that someone had managed to come in without my hearing them. No one. Either my imagination was piqued by my unusual surroundings, or the store was haunted. By the onion-scented ghost of a former owner, no doubt.

Heavy footsteps sounded, and I quickly put the book back and sat in the chair. "Sorry," Mr. Briggs said. He was a short man with a paunch and a yellowish, jaundiced cast to his skin, wearing gray slacks and a blue and gray argyle sweater vest over a white button-down shirt. A pair of very old-fashioned half-moon glasses perched on his blond head, apparently forgotten. "A long-time customer. We try to keep them happy, of course."

"Of course," I said, wondering at "we." Mr. Briggs, as far as I could tell, ran the shop alone. It was why I was there. "Do you do a lot of business online?"

"Not online," Mr. Briggs said. He pulled a metal stool that looked like the distant cousin of my chair around from behind the counter and sat, drawing his feet up to rest on the lower rung. "We deal strictly in the catalogue trade. Most of our customers don't use the internet at all."

"I see," I said, though I didn't, really. "So... phone calls, order forms...?"

"Exactly. And walk-in customers. We don't get as many of those these days. The neighborhood hasn't exactly gone downhill, but much of the foot traffic has been diverted west. People have to make an effort to reach us, which is probably to the good."

No organization. No customers. No desire for customers. And the place smelled strange. I clasped my hands in my lap, atop my purse. I ought to leave, thank him for his time and say I didn't think I was a good fit. But that would be rude. "I wasn't quite clear on the job description," I said. "What would my—the duties be?"

"Cash register, of course," Mr. Briggs said. "Stocking new inventory. Filling catalogue orders. Light cleaning. Then there's the opportunity to move up to customer relations. It's not very demanding work, but you'd start at fifteen dollars an hour and work your way up from there."

Fifteen. That was almost half again what I could make at the Pick 'n' Pack, which was my only other job lead so far. "It sounds interesting," I heard myself say.

"Then it's settled. How do you feel about starting now?"

I gaped. "Ah... don't you want to interview me?"

"No need. Your resume is exactly what we're looking for."

"But..." I felt, perversely, as if I should talk him out of it. "My resume is practically empty."

"Which means you don't have any bad habits to unlearn."

"That can't be a solid basis for hiring someone!"

"It isn't." Mr. Briggs took his glasses off his forehead and settled them firmly on his nose. "But our other criteria won't matter to you."

"I think I have a right to know what my qualifications are."

"All right. You're punctual, you're quiet, and you know how to type. Do you want the job or not?"

I wobbled on the chair again. "I do."

"Then I'll show you where you can put your things, and you can get started." Mr. Briggs stood and moved the stool back behind the counter. "Do you have any questions?"

I had so many questions I felt choked with them. Naturally, I came out with the most irrelevant one. "Abernathy's. The store. Who's Abernathy?"

Mr. Briggs smiled, making his cheeks puff up like a blond chipmunk's. "An excellent question," he said, and moved off into the stacks without saying anything more. I stood unmoving, confused, for a few seconds before remembering I was now an employee and shouldn't stand around gaping.

Mr. Briggs showed me the tiny room, barely more than a closet, that in any other store I would have called a break room. It contained a small folding table and a couple of those freezing metal chairs, a wooden coatrack with two of the pegs sheared off, and a miniature refrigerator and microwave. I reluctantly hung my coat on one of the remaining pegs—the place was still bitterly cold—and followed Mr. Briggs to the room opposite, which turned out to be his office. Stacks of cardboard boxes full of glossy catalogues stood waist-high against the far wall, tilting haphazardly against one another.

Mr. Briggs sat in a rolling office chair and leaned over to open the bottom drawer of the tan melamine and chrome desk. "This is the employee agreement," he said, coming up with a single sheet of paper. "We've never seen the point of a lot of paperwork. Read it first, if you want, but it's fairly basic. Then you sign *here* and *here*." He pushed the phone, putty-colored and older than I was, out of the way to lay the paper on the desk.

I read the document, which was handwritten in green ink. Abernathy's wasn't interested in my address, my Social Security number, my mother's maiden name, or anything else. There were just a few paragraphs outlining the job description Mr. Briggs had given me, a few more paragraphs in which I asserted that I wasn't a felon or a drug dealer, and then, bizarrely, a line that read *I, ______ , swear to uphold the standards of Abernathy's without fear or favor, and to seal its secrets in my heart, for as long as it remains in my charge.*

"What does this mean?" I asked.

"It means you won't disclose confidential information about our patrons," Mr. Briggs said. He had his eyes fixed on the document, not on me, and his fingers drummed restlessly on the melamine. I hesitated. "Is there a problem?"

"... No. No problem." I signed with the leaky plastic ballpoint he handed me, then gave pen and paper back to him and watched him countersign on the line below my signature.

He folded the paper in thirds and rolled backward to put it away in the top drawer of the filing cabinet. Then he unlocked the desk's middle drawer with a small brass key and opened it. "Mailing list," he said, handing me a sheaf of paper. "We send out a catalogue three times a year. You'll type the labels, address the catalogues, and have them ready for me to take to the post office tomorrow morning."

"All right," I said. The list was ten pages long and the addresses written in a cramped, faded hand. "Where's the computer?"

"No computer. We don't have any need for them." Mr. Briggs indicated a smaller desk behind his own. On it was an electric typewriter in a pebbly beige case. I'd seen ones like it before. In a museum.

"There are labels in a box in the filing cabinet. Let me know if you need anything else."

When he was gone, I took a catalogue from the topmost box and flipped through it. The glossy, slick cover had a blurred photo of the storefront under the name ABERNATHY'S. Someone stood next to the front door, possibly Mr. Briggs, though the photo was blurry enough it was impossible to tell.

Inside, there was no table of contents; lines of tiny print spread neatly in two columns across gray recycled paper. I ran my finger down the columns, accidentally smearing the cheap ink. I didn't recognize any of the titles, which weren't in alphabetical order. Some catalogue. I dropped it back into the box and regarded the antique typewriter with a sigh. All right, it wasn't all that antique, but forty years old was still old enough to qualify. I wasn't even sure I knew how to use it.

I found the labels and some blank white paper in one of the drawers of the filing cabinet. I practiced for a bit with the paper until I had the hang of the thing, then inserted the labels and started typing. For all the handwriting was crabby and small, it was easy to read, and I soon fell into a rhythm that let my brain wander pleasantly, far away from this store that smelled of onion.

My parents would be thrilled I'd gotten the job, though they'd be just as thrilled if I was working at the Pick 'n' Pack. What they wanted was for me to be employed, period, so I'd move out of their basement and become a responsible adult. Not that they were as blunt about it as that. They'd been generous in letting me pay rent and some of the grocery bill, and never nagged me about my future. I was lucky, really.

I came to the end of a sheet of labels and inserted a fresh one. My mind wandered away again. I was twenty-one years old; you'd think I'd have some idea what I wanted to do with my life. But I'd graduated from high school without making much of an academic splash, had made it through a couple of years of community college before the money ran out, and now... Well, this wasn't the best job in the world, but if I could stick it out, maybe get a raise—did Mr. Briggs offer benefits?—I might, at some point, come close to having a clue about my future.

I heard whispering again, and turned around fast, knocking the list to the floor. Nothing. I got up and opened the door. The hall outside was empty. I shut the door again and shook my head. I was being stupid. Just because the bookstore and Mr. Briggs were a little weird didn't mean I had to let my imagination come up with more weirdness. I was level-headed and not superstitious, and I was wasting time.

The mailing list had fallen splayed-out on the floor. I leaned over to pick it up, and a wave of dizziness struck me. For a moment, the room was outlined in flickering blue light. Then it passed, and I sat clutching the list in both hands. *That* had been strange. I bent over and sat up again, but felt nothing but a brief pressure as the blood rushed to my head and away again. The room looked perfectly normal. Shrugging, I spread out the mailing list again and resumed typing. I could ask Mr. Briggs... and have him decide his new employee was mentally unstable. It could stay a mystery.

By the time I reached the end of the mailing list, I was starving. I checked my watch. 1:17. I hadn't brought any food because I hadn't expected to start work immediately. There was a market around the corner. Mr. Briggs had to give me some sort of lunch break, right?

Mr. Briggs was gone when I left his office. I checked the break room and knocked tentatively on the washroom door; both were empty. I quickly used the toilet, which was as ancient as the typewriter, probably had one of those 3.5 gallon tanks that weren't legal anymore, washed my hands, and ventured into the bookstore proper. Most of the bookcases were knocked together out of plywood and lengths of unfinished yellow 2x8s, though there were a few proper cases of polished, chipped oak and two blackish-brown units that came from IKEA. I sidled between them, unwilling to call out Mr. Briggs' name into the silence of the store. The hush was so profound I imagined the books were sleeping.

Just as I'd begun a reverie about putting books down for a nap and imagining what kind of lullabies they would prefer, I heard the door open, then slam shut with such force it rippled through my skin. That couldn't possibly be Mr. Briggs. I hurried to the front of the store, feeling a sidelong sense of responsibility at being, as far as I could tell, the only Abernathy's employee on site. Then I felt embarrassed at my reaction. It was a store. People were supposed to come in and browse, Mr. Briggs' odd notions to the contrary. Even so, I probably shouldn't give anyone ideas about shoplifting.

The man was standing next to the counter when I emerged from the maze of bookcases, as if he'd been waiting for me. In his three-piece pinstriped suit, his handstitched leather shoes, and heavy gold watch, he looked as out of place in Abernathy's as a computerized cash register would be. He was studying his watch, but looked up when I arrived, and I felt caught by his dark-eyed gaze, pinned to the nearest case like a captive butterfly. "Who are you?" he said, somewhat irritably.

"Helena Davies. I started work this morning." I immediately wished I hadn't sounded so defensive.

Irritation gave way to surprise. "Nathaniel hired *you*? Impossible."

I swallowed a sharp response. *The customer is always right, especially when he could probably buy this whole store twice over*. "Can I help you with something?" I said, hoping he'd say no, because the only help I was capable of giving was directions to the toilet, which wasn't for public use.

"I doubt it," the man said. "Who *are* you?"

I regarded him more closely. He was good-looking, with fashionably styled dark hair, and no more than thirty, but he had an air about him that would have better suited an octogenarian with a Napoleon complex. "I don't know why you're so sure I don't belong here, but I'm certain I signed an employment contract," I said, trying not to think about how irregular the paperwork had seemed. "Maybe I should go get Mr. Briggs."

"You do that," the man said. "Nathaniel must be in the basement. Why don't you bring him here, and I can convince him to be sensible."

"I don't know—" I shut my mouth. I felt I'd already told this man too much. "Please wait here," I said, and backed away. Turning my back on him made me nervous.

I hadn't realized there was a third door beyond the office and the break room. It was flat plywood, stained dark like the walls of the short hallway, with an iron knob that looked like a black knot against the wood. I opened it to find stairs descending into perfect blackness. A string swayed in the faint breeze of the opening door, and I tugged on it, lighting a single dim bulb that didn't do much more than set shadows moving.

The steps were raw wood, splintered on the edges except where hundreds of feet had worn them smooth. They didn't creak under my weight, to my surprise; I'd almost expected the cries of the damned with every step. At the bottom of the stairs, there was a light switch. I flipped it on, and a couple of fluorescent bulbs flickered into life. They cast a brilliant light over the small, cold basement with its dark concrete floor. I looked down, and screamed.

Mr. Briggs lay face down a few feet from the foot of the stairs. Dark blood spread across the back of his argyle sweater and pooled beneath his chest and head. I stumbled forward and knelt beside him, scraping one knee on the cold concrete. His eyes were closed, and I fumbled at his throat for a pulse. I didn't know how to find a pulse. I didn't know how to do any of the things you were supposed to do to see if someone was alive. I leaned far forward, holding my hair out of the way, and put my cheek near his mouth. No warmth, no breath.

Someone thundered down the stairs. "Move back," the strange man said. I scooted back, tugging my skirt over my knees, and watched the stranger crouch over Mr. Briggs and repeat the same movements I'd made. Finally, he stood up and put his hands on his hips. "Nathaniel," he said. It sounded like a reprimand. As if Mr. Briggs was in trouble for being killed.

"What are you—we have to call the police!" I reached for my phone and came up empty. I'd left it in my purse—no pockets in this skirt. I felt my breath coming in quick, ragged pants and forced myself to stay calm.

"That would be a serious error," the stranger said. "Starting with the fact that you'd certainly be their first suspect."

I gaped at him, panic welling up again. "Are you crazy? Look, I don't have any blood on me, I hardly touched him! There's no reason to suspect me!"

"You were alone in the store with him, you are a new employee—you might have killed him to get at the contents of the cash box."

"Then why would I stay around to call for help?"

The man sighed. "I'm not saying they'd convict you. I'm saying they would make your life hell for a while. Is that what you want?"

I looked at him, at his height and the way he stood, and felt more chilled even than the basement could account for. "I... think I'll risk it." I took a few casual steps toward the stairs, never letting my eyes leave his face.

"I didn't kill him," he said, exasperated. "I don't have any blood on me either, do I? And I think whoever stabbed Nathaniel in the back would be at least a little bloody."

"How do you know that's what happened?"

He pointed. "There's a gash in the back of his sweater. You can see where the blood collected there first and made the fabric curl. Look, whoever you are, you can't be stupid or Nathaniel wouldn't have hired you. Somebody came into the store and killed Nathaniel, and you're damned lucky whoever it was didn't realize you were here, or you'd have joined him."

I sat down heavily on the second stair from the bottom, my vision clouding over. "They had to know I was here," I said. "That typewriter isn't quiet."

"It's not important," the man said. "What matters is we need to get someone to take care of Nathaniel's body. Someone who isn't the police."

"That's insane. We have to tell the police. People don't just 'take care of' dead bodies."

"The police will draw far too much attention to this store. No, we'll handle this matter privately. I'll need your permission to—"

"*My* permission? What do you mean, 'privately'? I'm calling the police."

The man focused on me then, his attention an uncomfortable knuckle digging into the base of my neck. "What's your name again?"

"Helena. Helena Davies."

"And you're certain Nathaniel hired you today?"

"Yes."

"Well, Helena Davies," the man said, his lips curving in a sardonic smile, "you've just inherited this bookstore."

2

I gaped at him again. "It doesn't work that way."

"Nathaniel didn't tell you *anything?*" The man shook his head. "Let's go upstairs. There's nothing we can do for him now, and this situation is more serious than I thought."

I felt too numb to keep arguing. I let him lead the way up the stairs as I turned off the lights, then, after a moment's thought, turned the single bulb back on. I don't know why the thought of leaving Mr. Briggs alone in the dark felt so wrong, but I couldn't bear to do it. I glared at the man, but he either didn't notice or didn't feel my moment of sentimentality mattered.

We went back to the front of the store, where the man pulled out a mobile phone that looked like it could exceed the speed of light and tapped the screen a few times. The phone made no noise, no beeping nor dialing sounds, but the man held it to his ear and, after a few silent seconds, said, "This is Campbell. Theta epsilon at Abernathy's." I heard the tiny distant sound of speech, then Campbell said, "That's what I said. Ask Lucia to come now." He lowered the phone, tapping the screen once to end the call.

"What was that about?" I said.

Campbell looked at me again, this time narrowly, assessing me. "I shouldn't be the one to tell you this," he said. "But I am, if nothing else, obedient to the Accords, and there doesn't seem to be anyone else. If Nathaniel—" He half-turned away, rubbing the bridge of his nose and pinching his lips tight against whatever words were trying to escape them. "I wish he was alive so I could throttle him," he continued in a low, rough voice. "This couldn't have happened at a worse time."

"Are you blaming him for getting killed?" I wished more than ever I dared slap his smug face.

"I'm blaming him for being so close-mouthed we might lose the most important resource we have in this war. Sit down. You look like you're about to faint."

"I'm not going to faint," I said, outraged, "but I'm thinking seriously about punching you in the face."

He raised an eyebrow. "Have I done something to offend you?"

"Treated me like a servant? Talked down to me? Acted like all of this is some huge cosmic plan to inconvenience you? No, of course not!"

To my irritation, he laughed. "You're not what I thought you were," he said. "I'll remember not to underestimate you again. You really do look like you need to sit down. I'll tell you what I can, which isn't much, I'm afraid, and then when Lucia arrives, she should be able to tell you more."

I sat on the freezing chair and clenched my hands in my lap. I wished I dared go back for my coat. It was really cold. But I was afraid if I left Campbell alone, he might leave, and then I'd never get answers to any of the questions that were multiplying in my brain.

"First, a proper introduction. My name is Malcolm Campbell, and I am a master of the... let's call them the magical arts."

"Magical arts," I said. "You're about to tell me you aren't a stage magician."

"I begin to see why Nathaniel hired you," Campbell said. "Real magic, not rabbits out of hats. Not that I haven't turned my hand to the latter sometimes."

"Prove it." Defying him felt good, like something I could control in all this madness.

"What would you accept as proof?"

I shrugged. The fog across my vision had cleared, leaving me feeling surreally alert, the way you do on a snowy morning when the sun is out and everything is outlined in clear, sharp, rainbow edges. Magic. Real magic. My employer was dead in the basement and this man was apparently part of some covert organization that used Greek letters as codes for things. I would humor the lunatic stranger for a few minutes, excuse myself, get my phone and call 9-1-1 as quickly as I could. "Do something no stage magician could do."

Campbell looked around. "Do you care about those books?" he said, indicating the stack of *Master Your Potential!* on the counter.

"Not really."

"Counting from the top, pick one."

"Four."

The top three books rose into the air to hover above the counter. The fourth book drifted casually toward me. I watched it come without interest. "It's done with wires," I said.

"That's not the magic. Or, rather, it *is* magic, but I don't expect you to be impressed by that."

I held out my hands to accept the book. On the dust jacket, a toothily smiling woman wearing some vaguely Indian robes and a lot of clunky gold jewelry held a glowing orb on her extended palm. "What *will* I be impressed by?"

"Examine the book. Touch it. Smell it. Make sure it hasn't been tampered with."

I rolled my eyes, but did as he said. It smelled of paper and ink and not much else. "What would it smell like if you'd tampered with it?"

"Something flammable," Campbell said. "Now, hold it on your palms, well away from you."

I stretched out my arms.

The toothy woman burst into flame.

I shrieked and jerked away, dropping the book. It hung in midair, then floated away from me, blazing hotter as it did. Campbell stood there, his arms crossed over his chest. "Tell me how I managed that," he said.

My panicked breathing slowed, not by much. "I don't know."

"It's a simple trick, but it *is* real magic. And believing that is the first step in understanding everything else you're going to learn this afternoon."

A speck of fire had burned a little spot of char into my skirt. It probably wouldn't be noticeable against the dark gray. "But *why?* Why are you telling me this?"

"Because you're now the custodian of Abernathy's."

"I'm not much more than a file clerk!"

"That's only because Nathaniel foolishly hired someone with no knowledge of what Abernathy's really is. If he'd done as he was supposed to do—I don't know what he was thinking. I didn't even know he was looking for an assistant. But that's irrelevant now. Abernathy's has no file clerks, it has custodians. People who know the books. Either you take this position, or—"

"So I have a choice. Fine. I choose to call the police and then take a job at the Pick 'n' Pack."

"Or Abernathy's shuts its doors, and the balance in this Long War tilts, and everything you care about may be destroyed," he said, as if I hadn't interrupted him.

"War?" I said.

"War. The details don't matter right now, given the situation we find ourselves in. What matters is the role Abernathy's plays in the fight."

"I suppose we're one of the good guys?" Belatedly, I realized I'd used the word "we," but Campbell shook his head.

"Abernathy's is a Neutrality," he said, and I could hear him emphasize the capital letter. "In the service of good, yes, but it's not as simple as good versus evil."

"Why not?"

"Again, not something that matters to you right now. Or should matter, really."

"I'm starting to once again feel the urge to punch you. Can't you just tell me the truth? It sounds like I'm involved whether I like it or not."

"I'm having trouble *not* telling you things that will unduly influence you." Campbell leaned up against the plywood counter, a relaxed move at odds with his elegant suit. "As I said, I'm obedient to the Accords, which lay out clearly the protections of the Neutralities. Lucia will explain it better, anyway."

"Who's Lucia?" He'd said it oddly, "loo-chee-ah."

"A custodian of a different Neutrality." Campbell came toward me, and I shot out of my chair, but he only moved to look out the glass of the front door. I headed toward the back of the store. "Miss Davies," he said, and despite myself, I stopped and turned to face him. He stood with his back to the door, putting his face in shadow, and his eyes were black smudges, expressionless.

"Miss Davies," he said, "if you call the police, I won't stop you. But you will open this store, and yourself, to influences that are a lot less friendly than I am. Someone murdered Nathaniel Briggs, and if that person was trying to attack Abernathy's, the murderer may feel you're also an acceptable target. You may not believe everything I'm telling you, you may not feel a responsibility to this store, but you're in this now, and the only way to protect yourself is to accept that."

I looked at the charred remains of the book, which now lay on the floor near the chair. The woman's grinning visage had been completely obliterated. The image of Mr. Briggs' dead body lying limp at the foot of the basement stairs came to mind, and with it the thought of an indistinct figure stabbing him from behind, creeping up the stairs and pushing open the door to the office. That typewriter was loud enough I wouldn't have heard anyone approach. I shuddered. "What do I do?"

Campbell didn't move, but I felt a tension go out of him. "For now, we wait," he said. "Lucia will be here shortly. She'll bring someone to remove the body discreetly and give you some basic instructions."

"Isn't there *anything* you can tell me? I'm not even sure that paperwork I filled out was legally binding!"

"Trust me, you're the one. Nathaniel is—was—nothing if not thorough. Ah, this is Lucia now."

A small white van pulled up to the curb in front of the store. It occurred to me that that spot had been empty when I arrived that morning and I was pretty sure it had stayed empty the whole time. That nearly convinced me of magic all by itself: empty parking spaces, even in this part of town, were rare.

I watched a woman and two men emerge and come toward the front door. Campbell backed away to give them room to enter. The woman was dark-haired and well-rounded, in her late forties probably, wearing a baggy sweat shirt and yoga pants in purple and bright pink. The two men had matching blond buzz cuts and wore jeans and plain T-shirts, one red, one black. They looked around the store curiously, scoping out new territory. The woman focused on me, and I had to keep myself from cringing, because her expression said I was an inconvenience she wished she could have the men get rid of.

"Theta epsilon?" she said. "I only came because I know it's impossible. No one uses those codes anymore." She had the faintest Italian accent.

"Nathaniel's dead, Lucia," Campbell said. He didn't seem fazed by her attitude. "In the basement."

"Who's she? A witness?" Lucia transferred her irritated gaze to Campbell. "Or a suspect?"

"She's Abernathy's new custodian."

"Impossible." Lucia looked me up and down again. "I would have known if Briggs had hired someone."

"I took the job just a few hours ago," I said, determined not to be cowed.

"Convenient," Lucia said. "Maxwell. Henry. Basement."

The two men headed off toward the back of the store. I hesitated briefly, then turned to follow them.

"You stay here," Lucia said.

Her tone of voice, like someone calling a dog to heel, broke through my intimidated stupor. "If I'm Abernathy's custodian," I said, "then I can't let strangers into the back unaccompanied. *You* can come with *me* if you want." And I turned my back on her and followed the men. I heard Campbell chuckle, then say something I couldn't make out. Well, Lucia already disliked me; I could hardly make things worse.

I waited at the top of the basement stairs while Maxwell and Henry examined Mr. Briggs' body for signs of life. Then one of them —it hadn't been clear who was who, from Lucia's instructions— produced a folded square of blue plastic tarp out of nowhere, maybe literally out of nowhere, and unfolded it until it looked large enough to cover the entire basement. The other gently lifted Mr. Briggs' body onto it, and together they wrapped him in the tarp until he looked like a blue plastic mummy. They managed to do this without getting any blood on themselves or on the outside of the tarp—more magic?

I backed out of their way as they brought their burden carefully upstairs. The whole thing had been done in silence, whether out of reverence for the dead or simply not needing to waste words, I wasn't sure.

Lucia and Campbell were where I'd left them, though they were having a conversation that cut off before we reached them. "Let me take care of this," Campbell said, and touched the bundle. It shimmered, then went solid again, and to me it still looked like a body wrapped in a tarp, but Lucia nodded and held the door open for the men. They opened the sliding door of the van, which turned out to have no seats aside from the two in front, and put their burden inside. This was all completely visible, but none of the passing cars slowed at all. Either people were more indifferent than I'd thought, or Campbell really had worked some kind of magic on the body. In which case, why hadn't I been affected?

One of the men climbed in with the body and shut the door. The other got in the driver's seat, and the little van pulled away from the curb and disappeared off down the street.

"That's settled," Lucia said. "Now, for you."

"Wait," I said. "Shouldn't someone have examined the body in place? For evidence?"

"No need," Lucia said. "We can learn everything we need to know at... somewhere else."

"You don't have to be cagey with her," Campbell said.

"I'm not convinced she's the right person," Lucia said.

I forgot, for the moment, that I felt the same way. "Why not?" I said, a little belligerently. "Mr. Briggs hired me."

"So you say. He didn't give you any instructions. He might just have wanted you for mundane tasks. Abernathy's does have those."

"It's simple enough to find out," Campbell said. "At least, so I've heard."

"Don't teach me my business, Campbell," Lucia said irritably. "All right. What's your name again?"

"Helena Davies."

"Go find me a book, Davies. Take one off a bookcase and bring it to me."

"What kind—"

"I don't care. Any kind. Hurry up, I've got things to do."

I turned on my heel and walked away, quickly, wanting nothing more than to get away from her. Then I kept walking, but more slowly, trying to imagine what kind of book would satisfy her. Why was the place so disorganized? How did—how *had* Mr. Briggs ever found anything? I scanned titles. Some of them weren't in English. Some of them weren't even in English script. There was no way I could guess what would interest Lucia. So I decided to choose one that interested me.

A blue binding, sky blue, in the middle of a row of black leather spines caught my eye. I pulled it off the shelf. It was hardbound, had no dust jacket, and the title, *Reflections*, was printed on the front cover but not on the spine. I flipped it open at random. The text was printed in double columns on each page, and the columns rather than the pages were numbered. It looked like an account of someone's travels in, I thought, southeast Asia. I loved books about travel.

I closed the book and returned to Lucia. She held out her hand for it, and I slapped it into her palm with a little too much force. She didn't flinch. She opened it to the title page and went still.

"You see?" Campbell said. He wasn't quite gloating.

"Do I pass?" I said.

Lucia looked up from the book. Then she turned it around so I could see the title page. *Reflections*, in big Gothic lettering, and below that, in smaller print, *Silas Abernathy*.

"Abernathy," I said. "Is that a coincidence?"

"Silas Abernathy used to run this store," Campbell said.

That shook me. "I didn't know," I said. "I got lucky."

"That's not how the store works," Lucia said. "Did you feel anything strange earlier? Change in your vision, dizziness?"

"Sort of. There was a moment when the whole room seemed filled with blue light. I thought it was a head rush."

Lucia closed the book and handed it back to me. "Briggs keeps—kept a spare ring of keys in his desk drawer. You'll need those."

"Why?"

She sighed, and suddenly she was just a very tired middle-aged woman, not at all terrifying. "Abernathy's hasn't closed mid-day in over a hundred and fifteen years," she said, "but you can't be left to tend it, uninformed and unprepared. One hour, and I'll tell you what I can in that time. Then it's up to you."

"Can't it be faster? I need an augury," Campbell said.

"You'll have to wait."

"How long?"

"Campbell, haven't you learned patience yet? Come back tomorrow." Lucia pushed open the door and made a little shooing gesture with her free hand. Campbell said something under his breath, glaring at Lucia, but left the store.

I was about to follow him when he turned back toward me. "Miss Davies," he said, "take care. The murderer is still out there. I'll see you in the morning."

"Um... goodbye," I said, but he was already getting into his car, a vintage silver Jaguar parked a few spaces down the road from the store. It was exactly the sort of car I'd have expected him to drive. He made a three-point turn, forcing another car to stop and honk at him, then drove away in the direction opposite the one the van had gone. I watched until he turned a corner out of sight, and felt stupid for feeling bereft. It said something about the day I'd been having that Malcolm Campbell had become comforting and familiar.

3

Lucia cleared her throat, and I startled.

"The keys, Davies," she said, and before I could stop myself I let her peremptory voice propel me back inside to the office, where I set the blue book down on Mr. Briggs' desk. As I rooted around in the desk for a ring of keys, my eye fell on the stack of boxes. *I'll have to mail those out soon,* I thought, and had enough time to be stunned by how casually I'd assumed responsibility for the catalogues before I found the keys. There were five of them, attached to a keychain made from an alligator's foot, dried out and horrible. I hoped it didn't have mystic significance.

Lucia waited impatiently as I fumbled around, trying to work out what key fit the front door, and hung an ancient CLOSED sign in the front window. Then she stalked through the store like a bird of prey hunting a mouse, her eyes darting everywhere. It made me nervous for a completely different reason; I felt sure Mr. Briggs would have objected to her being in the back rooms of Abernathy's. But I didn't think I had much choice.

She went directly for the break room, like she'd known where it was, and dropped heavily into one of the folding chairs. I took a seat opposite her.

Lucia didn't speak for a long time. Her eyes were bright blue, startling against her darkly tanned skin, and her short brown hair curled up at the ends. I stared back at her, wondering what she saw when she looked at me: dark blond hair caught up in a ponytail I hoped looked professional, brown eyes like my father's, a mouth that crooked on one side like my mother's. Finally, she said, "Why did you apply for work here?"

"I saw the ad in the paper," I said. Actually, it had been my father who saw it. When I'd said something about nobody placing want ads in the newspaper anymore, he said "Then you'll be the only one who applies, right?"

"A newspaper ad," Lucia said disgustedly. "What was he thinking?"

"Was he supposed to do something different?" I asked.

Lucia waved that away. "So you just walked into the store and Briggs gave you the job. Did he say why?"

"He said something about how I didn't have any bad habits to unlearn."

"Well, at least he wasn't completely out of his mind. Why did you take the job?"

"It pays well, and it seemed interesting. Working in a bookstore, I mean. Are you going to keep grilling me, or do I get some information?"

Lucia's lips thinned, pressed tight together in a straight line. "This has never happened before in all the years of Abernathy's existence. Every custodian has come to the position with years of instruction behind them. And now you walk through the door and end up—" She pushed her chair back, but didn't stand. I didn't move. I had the feeling if I said or did anything, I'd lose my chance at understanding what the hell was going on.

"You're going to have trouble believing what I'm about to tell you," Lucia said.

"If it's about magic being real, Mr. Campbell already convinced me of that."

"Typical. Campbell's got no sense of self-preservation. For all he knew, you might have gone running off to tell the world what you'd seen."

"I don't think it's that much of a risk. Who'd believe me if I said I'd seen someone light a fire with magic?"

"You'd be surprised. But it doesn't matter. You know magic is real. What else did he tell you?"

"That there's a war going on."

"That's true. This world is at war," Lucia said. "It has been at war for nearly seven hundred years with creatures beyond your imagining—alien in every sense. What do you know about parallel universes?"

"Isn't that science fiction?"

"Yes. But the idea is useful. We are at war with creatures who come from somewhere outside our reality, but the thing is, we don't understand where that place is."

"What do you mean, outside our reality? Like, some kind of dreamland?"

"Nightmareland would be more accurate. For a long time, we believed it was Hell, and the creatures were demons, but the Enlightenment taught us otherwise. And no, I don't know whether there really is a Heaven or a Hell. Theology isn't my idiom."

Since I'd been about to ask that question, I decided shutting up was still the best policy.

"Anyway. Calling it a parallel universe is as close to the truth as humanity can fathom, even though it's a false analogy. Whatever or wherever it is, it's a reality that produces monsters that invade our world regularly. These invaders want what we have and they are willing to kill us to get it."

"And that is...?"

"Magic."

She leaned back in her chair, examining me closely. I had no idea what she was looking for—shock? Disbelief? Horror? Well, it was too late for shock; Campbell's magical fire had taken care of that. I knew too little about what she was talking about to be horrified by it. And disbelief... I always hated it in books where the heroine is presented with evidence of a mystical world and then spends the next two hundred pages insisting it's all a hoax. "You mean... Like some kind of natural resource?" I said.

Her eyes widened briefly in surprise, like she'd asked a question she didn't think I knew the answer to. "Like that," she said. "They need magic to survive. So do we. Our survival depends on winning this war."

"That sounds dire." I regretted my words instantly. They sounded more flippant than I felt. Lucia's expression went cold.

"This is not a joke," she said. "Men and women die every day, casualties of the war. The Wardens fight and they, too, die."

"And the Wardens are... magical guardians?"

"Yes." Lucia scowled. "You're going to misunderstand what I'm about to tell you."

"I'm not stupid."

"It's not about being stupid. Just... listen, and don't jump to any conclusions." She took a breath. "All humans are sources of magic. It flows through us like... you've already started thinking mystically."

"It sounds mystical. Like—"

"If you say 'like the Force,' I'm walking out of here. It's not mystical. It's just a thing that is. Magic fills us, like... it's not too wrong to think of it as similar to blood. Having it doesn't make us capable of doing magic. People can't use their magic any more than you could make your blood more oxygenated by thinking about it. But we need it to survive. So when an invader drains someone of their magic, they die."

I kept my mouth shut. Any questions I'd ask would no doubt be stupid ones, and maybe if I stayed quiet, I'd eventually understand.

"At any rate," Lucia went on, "Human beings are born incapable of wielding magic. That leaves us vulnerable to the invaders, who use magic as easily as you locked the front door. Wardens take the fight to the invaders, using magic and whatever other resources we can provide. Like Abernathy's. It's a weapon, and now, apparently, it is in your hands."

"Mr. Campbell said it was a Neutrality," I said. "That doesn't sound like a weapon."

Lucia made an indelicate snorting sound. "The war is not the only conflict. Some seventy years ago there was a rift within the Wardens. A disagreement as to how the war should be fought. Now the two groups fight each other almost as much as they do the invaders. Abernathy's is neutral in the matter. You're expected to treat each side as equals, regardless of your personal feelings."

"I don't have any personal feelings. I don't know anything about it!"

"You will."

"What's the disagreement?"

Lucia sighed. "Seventy-three years ago, Marie Nicollier discovered a way to capture and bind an invader that would allow a magus—someone who's undergone a ritual that changes them to make wielding magic possible—to control the invader's own magic. Force it to fight for us. The disagreement was over whether this was a good idea."

"It sounds unsafe."

"It *is* unsafe. It's also a huge advantage. But it doesn't matter to us."

"'Us'? That sounds like you've made up your mind."

"Briggs was a fool to drag an outsider into this, but your appointment is legitimate. You're now the custodian of Abernathy's, God help you."

"What does that mean?"

Lucia stood. "Come with me," she said.

We left the break room and went back into the bookstore. "What do you know about indeterminacy?" Lucia asked.

"I don't—you mean, like in quantum physics? I know it has something to do with Schrödinger's cat." I'd seen Neil deGrasse Tyson talk about it once on TV. Why did she keep coming up with scientific questions? "Could be alive, could be dead, don't know until you open the box."

"That's close enough. Abernathy's maintains a state of indeterminacy by never organizing anything. No one knows what's in here, therefore anything could be in here."

"But what about the catalogue? Isn't that a record of what's in the store?"

"The catalogue is different, and not the point right now. Did you want an explanation or not?"

"I'll shut up."

Lucia stopped and turned to face me. "What Abernathy's is," she said, "is the greatest oracle since the disappearance of the lady at Delphi. People come here asking for an augury or a prophecy, and you find them a book that answers their question. Not by knowing what they want, but by letting the store work through you."

I gaped at her. "That's impossible," I said, forgetting my resolve about not being *that girl* from the fantasy novels. "I'm not an oracle. I can't do anything like that."

"You're not the oracle, the store is." Lucia sounded irritated again. "But it needs hands to carry out its work. You're the hands."

It was too much. "I accept that there's magic," I said, "because I saw it. I believe you're telling the truth about the war, because what's the point of playing that kind of joke on a complete stranger? But this —it doesn't make any sense! These books couldn't possibly have been written with just one reader in mind!"

"I don't know how it works, so don't get snippy with me, Davies." Lucia took hold of a book and half-pulled it off the shelf, rocking it back and forth on its base. "How straightforward do you think prophecy is? People don't just receive a book and read out exactly the answer they came for. They have to work at understanding it."

"So I can take a book—"

"Not you. Custodians of the Neutralities can't use their magic on their own behalf."

"Why not?"

"It's part of the Accords. If you became a Nicollien sympathizer, or a Ambrosite, you could circumvent the limits placed on Abernathy's to give information to that faction. We're meant to be neutral."

"What does your Neutrality do?"

"I'm the custodian of the Gunther Node. It's a source of magic that magi can siphon in wielding magic."

"I thought they were called Wardens."

"Magi are people who can wield magic. People fighting the war are called Wardens. Becoming a magus doesn't mean you have to be a Warden, even though almost all of them are, and not all Wardens can wield magic. Get it?"

"Sure." Surprisingly, I did. "But—then you can ask it who killed Mr. Briggs!"

Lucia shook her head. "I told you it's not that straightforward. Abernathy's won't answer questions beginning with 'who'. Or anything else requiring a direct answer. We don't know if it can't, or if it's just stubborn. Either way, it's totally unhelpful in our current situation."

So much for that thought. "So how do I... when someone comes in looking for a prophecy, what do I do?"

Lucia smiled. It wasn't a nice smile. "I have no idea. Maybe there are instructions somewhere in here. But you'll have to figure it out on your own."

"But—"

Lucia pushed up her sleeve and ostentatiously looked at her watch. "Time's up," she said. "The rest is up to you. Abernathy's is open from ten in the morning to six at night, every day except Sunday. You have to be on the premises during that time. Good luck."

I followed her to the front of the store. "But... I thought you said Abernathy's was important! I don't know what I'm doing!"

"You'll figure it out," Lucia said, and the door banged shut behind her.

I realized my hand was clenched on the edge of the counter, the plywood cutting into my palm. I jerked my hand away quickly and shook the blood back into it. My eye fell on the charred remains of the book, and I bent to pick it up. It smelled of the ash that crumbled and shifted as I tilted the book, raining down onto the cracked linoleum to make new pale stars there. My hands began trembling, and I had to set the book down or drop it. I caught hold of the counter and shook uncontrollably. I'd seen a murdered man, I'd seen fire come from nothing, I'd been told... it was all too much.

I stared sightlessly at the glass countertop until the shaking passed. Then I stood up straight and brushed ash off my skirt. I wanted to believe it was all a joke, that maybe my father had set me up—he liked a good practical joke, he might have put the ad in the paper—but in my heart, I knew it was true.

There was magic, real magic, in the world.

And I was a part of it.

I spent the rest of the afternoon exploring the store. One of the keys was a second key to the front door. Another, an elaborate, lacy thing, locked the cash register, which turned out to contain about two hundred and fifty dollars in small bills. On a shelf below the register was a long, narrow book bound in gray leather, about half an inch thick. Inside, the pages were divided into three columns, and there were rows and rows of neatly lettered entries, each with a five-digit number, a name, and a date. The most recent date was yesterday. The five-digit numbers were consecutive. I set it aside to puzzle over later.

I did some poking around and discovered another door, this one leading to a side alley; it opened reluctantly, as if it had been closed for a century. The alley it opened on was narrow, barely big enough for two people to walk side by side, and certainly not big enough for large shipments. I hauled it closed and locked it again. Whoever had murdered Mr. Briggs hadn't come through that way.

Mr. Briggs' desk—my desk, now, and the thought made me shake again for a few seconds—was neatly organized. The brass key he'd used to unlock the middle drawer lay in a shallow tray in the long, narrow top drawer, along with pens, pencils, paper clips, and other basic office supplies. I unlocked the middle drawer; it was empty. After a moment's thought, I put the mailing list away and locked the drawer. Maybe something around here would give me some idea as to why it had to be protected.

The file cabinet wasn't locked, but it took me some effort to get the drawers open, because they were overflowing with papers jammed into manila folders. Some were yellowing and ancient, others were as bright as if they'd been filed yesterday. I slid one of the folders halfway out, careful to keep its spot in the drawer, and fanned through the papers. Each one had the name ABERNATHY'S printed in bold sans-serif font at the top, with what looked like a ledger drawn in crisp black ink below. The first one I looked at had *Alice Greenacre* written in a fancy, more elegant script above the ledger, and below that a line printed in neat block letters that read:

34874 aug. pers. Devil In Hand $5000 pd. cash & trade—12-07-1949

That made no sense. I glanced through a few others and realized the filing cabinet was probably the only thing in Abernathy's that was organized: the pages were all alphabetized by surname. Some ledgers were full, some had only one entry, but all followed the same pattern.

I took a closer look. Well, the first numbers were five digits long, which reminded me of the ledger book by the register. And the last numbers were probably dates. So, dated transactions. "$5000 pd. cash & trade," that was definitely a receipt. Not that I knew what "trade" meant, but it could be exchanging old books for new ones, since this was a bookstore. And "Devil In Hand" could be a title—all of them looked like titles. That made sense too.

I had no idea what "aug. pers." meant—"august personage"? No, that sounded dumb. And sometimes it was "aug. spec." or "aug. fam." and I had no guesses about those. But I had a fair idea these were Abernathy's records of purchased books. Did people really pay cash for prophecies? It seemed so mundane. Suddenly I wished Campbell would show up again. He'd behaved as if all this was perfectly normal, like he'd come for a prophecy a hundred times before. He could be as arrogant and snobbish as he wanted, as long as he helped me figure all this out.

Inspired, I ran my fingers across the folders until I found *Campbell, Malcolm*. Then I hesitated, feeling uncomfortable. Wasn't it a little like spying, reading his records? I scowled and pulled the folder out all the way. If he came back, and bought a book, I'd have to write it down—I'd briefly wondered if it was magic that wrote the records, but there were too many different handwritings for that to be likely—

and I'd see his other purchases then even if I didn't look now. Besides, how secret could they be?

There was only one sheet of paper in the folder, which was common; there weren't many folders with more than one ledger page. His name was written in a slightly less nice cursive script than most of the others, and there were only three entries, all labeled *aug. spec.*, each dated a year apart starting four years before. Method of payment: *sang. sap.*, whatever that meant. Each of them had been worth less than $1000. Expensive books, or cheap prophecies?

I put Campbell's folder away and checked the other drawers, hoping for some kind of manual, delaying the moment when I'd have to go back into the basement. I wasn't superstitious—much—but I couldn't stop seeing Mr. Briggs' body, covered in blood and lying so still it was clear he was dead. In the bottom drawer—I gasped and slammed it shut before cautiously opening it again. It was *full* of cash—neatly bundled fifties and hundreds, more than I could count at a casual glance. It made no sense. If someone had murdered Mr. Briggs for this—and it was enough to be worth murdering over—why hadn't they come into the office for it?

I closed the drawer again, shuddering, and examined the rest of the room. There were a few photos on the walls, showing the city as it had been in the thirties or early forties, judging by the dress of the people in them. One was the original of the blurry photo on the catalogue, less blurry; I'd had my back to it while I typed and hadn't noticed it before. The man in the photo was clearly bald under his hat and wore a three-piece brown suit.

I ran my finger along the top of the frame. It came away clean. Light cleaning, Mr. Briggs had said. Cleaning was a nervous habit of mine, not exactly something I enjoyed, but suppose Abernathy's was aware enough to know when it was dirty? An *intelligent* bookstore, that was another surprise for the day.

There was a closet at the far end of the office. I turned the knob and discovered it was locked. I examined the final key, then inserted it into the lock. It turned smoothly, and I opened the door to discover a tiny, windowless room. The back wall was unfinished brick, and I could see an outline where a doorway had been filled in. Occupying one side of the room was a flight of stairs, leading up.

I stepped through the door and looked up the stairwell. Late afternoon light from the landing window, blue and still, illuminated the stairs, which were uncarpeted and pale in places from years of wear. They were also coated thinly with dust. I took a few steps up and winced at the creak, which echoed in the otherwise still air as if the stairs themselves were challenging me. I kept going, trailing my fingers along the wall because there was no rail. The dark wainscoting was poorly stained and streaky in places, the smooth white plaster above felt cool and damp and slightly gritty, and I checked my fingertips to see if it was coming off on my hands. I rounded the corner of the landing and continued to ascend.

There was a door at the top, painted white with an oval iron knob and a keyhole. I tried the knob; locked. I hesitated, then took out the key that had opened the "closet" below. It wouldn't go in. I tried a couple more times, thinking it might only be stuck, but no, it wasn't the right key for the lock. For some reason, this spooked me more than Mr. Briggs' body had. Anything might be behind the door.

I jingled the keys. This was all fascinating, and incredibly mysterious, but what I needed was *information*. I should be looking in the store—

My heart lurched. I ran down the stairs and into the office. Did those back stairs count as part of the premises? Had I left the store open to anyone—or to the murderer, come back to finish the job?

4

I locked the door as quickly as I could with trembling hands and took a few careful steps into the store, listening. I heard nothing but my own breathing, which was quick and terrified. That meant nothing, if someone had already concealed himself in the store.

I searched among the bookcases for intruders, wishing I had something more dangerous on me than my phone, but found no one. So I went to sit behind the front counter, clasping my hands in my lap, and stared out the front window. I ought to search the basement, but at that moment nothing could make me go back down there. It could wait until tomorrow.

Cars slid past the plate glass window with ABERNATHY'S stenciled at the top, the letters reversed from my point of view. The sun had mostly set, coloring the world blue and gold, and I leaned my chin on my hand and tried not to think about how hungry I was. I hadn't eaten lunch, and it was well on the way to dinnertime. Mom was making lasagna for dinner, rich with ground beef and tomatoes and four kinds of cheese. My stomach rumbled again, and I checked my phone. Thirty-seven minutes, and I could lock up and go home.

The door slammed open. If there had been bells over it, they would have gone flying. "You," a young woman said, and slammed the door shut behind her. "Who do you think you are?" She was pretty in a petite, slender way, with dark hair cut pixie-style, close to her head, and round, rosy cheeks. I'd never seen eyelashes as long as hers before and wondered if they were fake. She wore a Jackie Kennedy pink wool coat and a knitted gray scarf that wrapped twice around her throat and fell past her waist.

"Helena Davies," I said. "Who are you?"

"Judy Rasmussen," the girl said. "What did you do? Trick Nathaniel into giving you the job?"

"Um, no." I sat up straight, wishing I'd put on lipstick that morning. Judy Rasmussen's makeup was perfect, just like the rest of her, and it made me, rumpled by my search of the store, feel unkempt by comparison. "He placed an ad, I answered it, he hired me. That's all."

"That job wasn't his to give away. I'm supposed to be Abernathy's next custodian. There's been a mistake."

She was giving me the same look Campbell and Lucia had given me, that same disdainful, you-can't-possibly-be-worthy look, and it made me angry.

"Lucia confirmed I'm the custodian. So it can't be that much of a mistake. I'm sorry if you're upset—"

"'Upset' isn't the word for it. It shouldn't take long to straighten this out. You're not a Warden, are you? All this must be a huge shock. I'm sure you know you don't belong."

"Meaning I'm not good enough?"

Judy gave me a once-over that Malcolm Campbell would have been proud of. "Why would you even want to be Abernathy's custodian when you don't know anything about it?"

"Because I..." It was a good question. I didn't have an answer.

Judy crossed her arms over her chest. "Look. It's simple. Tomorrow, you can abdicate, and go back to your own life. You don't understand what you've gotten mixed up in." She sounded sincere, not sneering, and it struck home. I *didn't* fully understand what was going on with Abernathy's and magic and the war. This *wasn't* my life.

"Abdicate?" I said.

"It's not hard. My father can take care of it in the morning. Look. I've been training for this for years. Do you really want a job you're not prepared for?"

It was another good question. Two hours ago, I would have said *I don't* and walked out the door, let Lucia deal with the fallout. But walking through the store had made me feel unexpectedly connected to all of this. "Mr. Briggs thought I was worthy. And I think you'd have to admit he had the right to choose."

Judy scowled. "Everyone knew who the next custodian was supposed to be."

"Apparently *everyone* was wrong. Maybe you ought to wonder why Mr. Briggs changed his mind. Maybe you aren't as perfect for the job as you think."

It was, as the saying goes, a palpable hit. Judy's eyes narrowed into black-fringed slits. "You don't know who you're talking to."

"I don't. Should I?"

"My father," Judy said, "is William Rasmussen."

"Sorry, that still doesn't mean anything to me."

"It will tomorrow," Judy said. "I guarantee it." She slammed back out the door, trapping the end of her scarf, and opened it abruptly to free it. I smiled, but it faded fast. Judy Rasmussen. William Rasmussen. I'd been casual about my ignorance, but the truth was I did feel nervous. Judy didn't seem like the kind of woman who'd make idle threats. Whoever William Rasmussen was, he was no doubt powerful enough to make my life miserable in some way. Well, I was sure he couldn't force me to step down as custodian, or Judy would have said as much, and I could deal with everything else. I hoped.

It was seven minutes to six. I went back through the store, making sure all the doors were locked and all the lights were out. I stood for a full minute looking down into the basement from the top of the stairs. The dangling bulb was the only light, so I could barely see the edge of the bloodstain where Mr. Briggs had lain. Something else to worry about in the morning.

The blue-bound *Reflections* by Silas Abernathy still lay atop the office desk. I flipped open the cover, then closed it. Maybe it wasn't an oracle, or a prophecy, or whatever you called it, but I'd chosen it, or it had chosen me, and I did like travel books. I picked it up and carried it with me out of the office. I'd borrow it, and put it back in the morning.

I locked the outer door at exactly one minute past six o'clock and dropped the keys into my purse along with the book. The store's windows looked back at me like empty eyes. I no longer felt the sense of connection I had earlier, just a dullness of spirit I told myself was hunger. The upper windows were curtained except for a sliver of darkness between two drapes. Maybe I should get a locksmith to let me through that secret door. Or maybe I should stop being so nosy. I sighed and turned away. If I hurried, I could catch the bus, and go home to eat a big piece of lasagna, and pretend my life was normal.

The bus ride home felt like it took forever. I sat huddled into my coat and watched the people around me. What did it mean that everyone was a source of magic? It didn't show on the outside, if that was true—unless it did show, and nobody knew to associate whatever it was with magic. The young bearded man wearing the knit cap and red plaid lumberjack's coat, wires trailing from his ear buds... the middle-aged mother sitting with her hand on her pre-teen son's knee... the white-haired guy who had paper grocery bags at his feet, overflowing with a head of celery and some loaves of sliced square bread... If Lucia was telling the truth, all of them were filled with magic, and none of them knew it. *I* was filled with magic. I didn't feel any different. Lucia had been so matter-of-fact about it, it made me wonder what else I didn't know.

My parents lived near Happy Valley in a ranch-style house with a daylight basement and a one-and-a-half car garage that only one car could fit into, even if it wasn't crammed full of the remnants of Mom's enthusiasms. I went in through the side door as usual, and walked into the warmth and delicious smells of my mother's kitchen. "Close the door!" Mom said. She was bent over the oven, removing a glass casserole dish that sent up waves of hot tomatoey goodness through the air.

"You're just in time," my brother, Jake, said. He was seated at the table with his feet up on the next chair, playing on his phone. "Set the table."

"It wouldn't kill you to help out," I said, swatting his legs to make him move.

"I'll lose my life."

"That could happen literally."

"Stop arguing and set the table, both of you," Mom said, setting the lasagna down. "Did you get the job?"

"They wanted me to start immediately." I hung my coat and purse up and took plates out of the cupboard. "It pays well and..." I couldn't think what else to tell her. Certainly not that I was working for an oracular bookstore, fighting a magical battle against alien invaders.

"Do you get benefits?" said my father, entering the room. He'd removed his tie and rolled up the sleeves of his blue and tan checked shirt. "That can be worth more than a paycheck, in this economy."

"I... think so. There's still a lot I don't know. But it's a position with... a lot of responsibility, and the work is interesting."

Jake tossed flatware on the table with a clatter. "It's a bookstore. How interesting can it be?"

"More interesting than getting creamed by guys the size of buffaloes six days a week." Jake, a junior, had made varsity this year and never let anyone forget it.

"It's winter, dummy," Jake said. He dropped into his seat and began heaping his plate with green salad. "Weight training."

"Fine. More interesting than seeing who can bench five hundred pounds." Though secretly I thought being able to bench press that much would be interesting.

"Let's not argue, all right?" Mom pushed the lasagna toward Dad so he could serve. It was such an old-fashioned gesture that I was once again struck by that sense of dissociation between past and present. My family *was* a little old-fashioned. Dad's job supported the family, even its hapless middle child. Mom had stayed home to take care of us when we were young and now had her own online business selling knitted children's clothing. None of us children had ever rebelled more seriously than my older sister Cynthia getting her eyebrow pierced when she was fourteen. We were normal, we were boring, and I liked it that way.

"It's not an argument, just a discussion," Jake said. "I want Helena to have a good job so she can move out and I can set up a big-screen TV in her room."

"We already have a big-screen TV downstairs," Dad said.

"This would be so I can have parties in private."

"That's never going to happen," Mom said. "Helena, what are your hours?"

"Well, it's six days a week, ten to six, and I'm not sure what kind of time off I get," I said, forking up lasagna and blowing on it to cool it.

"That's a lot of hours. Are you sure it's not too much?"

"Helena knows what she's doing, Louise," Dad said. "That still leaves time for socializing."

"With Viv," Jake said with a grin. Mom made a face. She'd disliked Viv ever since the time in third grade I came home from her house with my hair dyed bright Kool-Aid red. It didn't matter that it was temporary color; Viv represented randomness and chaos, things Mom hated nearly as much as imitation vanilla flavoring and press-on nails.

I took another bite. Rich, flavorful tomato sauce filled my mouth, cheese trailed from my fork to my lips, and I closed my eyes in bliss. My mother had spent most of my childhood taking cooking classes and trying the results on her family. Last night it had been Thai noodles in peanut sauce. Tomorrow it might be chicken cordon bleu. If she was hoping to encourage me to move out and become independent, her cooking wasn't helping her cause. "This is really good," I mumbled. Mom beamed.

Across the room, my phone buzzed from inside my purse. I made a move toward it. "Sit," Dad said. "You know the rules. No phones during dinner."

"It's probably Viv. I have to tell her I'm not interested in hanging out tonight." Socializing after the day I'd had would be exhausting.

"Doesn't Viv have a job?" Mom said. "It's Thursday. Even she can't be thinking of partying on a work night."

"She's waitressing mornings and plays gigs some evenings."

Mom made another face. Instability, the kind represented by Viv's efforts at making a name for herself as a musician, was another thing she hated. My phone buzzed again. "It could be urgent," I said.

"Everything's urgent to Viv," Dad said. "Enjoy your meal. Savor it. Stop rushing around. Kids these days, it's like they're surgically attached to their electronics." He was grinning the way he always did when he delivered one of his "kids these days" statements.

"I put *my* phone in my room," Jake said. I kicked him under the table.

In the kitchen, Mom's phone rang. "That's Cynthia," she said, and half-rose from the table.

"No phones," I said. She rolled her eyes at me, but sat back down. "Besides, she just wants to tell you about her latest big deal and how important she is."

"Be nice. Your sister has a right to be proud of her successes."

I shrugged. Cynthia and I had never gotten along, and even though our parents never compared me to her, I always felt them wondering why I didn't have goals and direction and a growing stock trading career and a hot boyfriend. Though they probably *didn't* think about the last; as far as my father was concerned, none of the guys we dated were good enough for his daughters.

I finished my lasagna and cleared my place, rinsed off the plate and put it into the dishwasher. "I'm downstairs if anyone wants me," I said, taking my phone and Silas Abernathy's book out of my purse. I trotted down the narrow stairs that now reminded me uncomfortably of the basement stairs of Abernathy's, complete with the dim glow of the light fixture. I crossed the basement without turning on the light and pushed my door open, kicking my shoes off and rubbing my toes in the thick pile of the carpet.

We'd moved into the house when I was three, and the purple

carpet had been there at the time. When I was ten, I'd started begging to have it replaced. By the time I was sixteen, I was used to it, and now I couldn't imagine my room without it. I fell onto my unmade bed face first, breathing in the smell of the lavender potpourri my mother scented the sheets with. So long as it smelled fresh, I didn't worry about making the bed. No point, when I was just going to mess it up again at night.

I rolled onto my back and stretched. My bookcase, with its top two shelves crammed with stuffed animals I couldn't bear to get rid of, loomed over me. Beside it hung a pair of matched Oriental prints: a woman demurely wielding a parasol and a robed man with his hand on a samurai sword. Sappy bunny eyes stared down at me. I made a face at Mr. Hoppy and took a look at my phone. Two texts from Viv.

WHERE R U

U COME TONITE RD PRL

I transferred my scowl to my phone. Viv meant the Red Pearl pub, and what she wasn't saying was "I got us both dates, come or die." Viv was my best friend, but she had this idea that it was her duty to find me a man now that I'd finally wised up and dumped Chet, and since she was the one who'd hooked me up with Chet in the first place, I felt her judgment was suspect.

I texted back NOT TONIGHT. TIRED FROM NEW JOB.

A few seconds later, she replied, YOU GOT JOB MUST CELEBRATE!

I groaned. If Viv was willing to spell words out and use punctuation, she might be hard to ditch. TOMORROW. I'M BEAT. SORRY.

Bzzt bzzt. YOU WILL BE. VY HOT GUYS

TOMORROW, VIV.

There was a longer pause. FINE U OWE ME

I wasn't sure I did, but I wasn't going to argue with her. I tossed my phone at my bedside table, but it missed and skidded across the surface to fall to the floor. I bent to pick it up and knocked something else onto the floor with my hip. The Abernathy book. I picked that up, too, and sat up to look at it more closely. The blue binding looked as fresh as if it had just come from the printer's, but the edges of the pages were brown-speckled with age. I opened it to the title page, then flipped a few more pages, looking for a table of contents or something that might give me an idea what this book was about.

There wasn't anything like that. Instead, the book began with *Chapter One* on the page following the title page. It was, as I'd seen before, arranged with two columns on each page and a number beneath each column rather than a page number. *Well, Dear Reader, it's nice to meet you,* I read. *I shouldn't have asked Warren to request the augury that predicted your existence, but I've already broken so many guidelines I don't lose sleep over that one. I hope you won't think less of me for it, young lady.*

My face tingled. He couldn't possibly be addressing me, could he? I thought back over everything I'd experienced that afternoon. No, it was entirely possible.

I don't know your name, or what prompted you to pick up this book, but I'd like to think we have a connection over the years. Whether you are a Warden, or a curious bystander, I also don't know. But I have a strong feeling that Abernathy's won't let this book go to just anyone, so for now I'll assume you're involved in the Long War in some capacity. Wouldn't it be a surprise to both of us if you're a custodian?

I closed the book with a snap and dropped it on my bed, curling my fingers around the blanket and squeezing so tightly it hurt. Fine. So I was custodian of Abernathy's, for now anyway. But this book... it was meant for someone who understood what was going on. It felt like spying, reading Silas Abernathy's cheerful account. He hadn't anticipated an outsider getting her hands on it. Or had he?

On the other hand... I was involved now, and anything I could learn would benefit me. At the very least it might help me make an informed decision about whether or not I should remain Abernathy's custodian. I picked the book up, ran my fingers along the spine, then opened it.

You should know I'm not the most reputable of characters. But then, if you're one of us, you've probably already heard the dozens of stories attached to my name. Silas Abernathy, war-time deserter, is the most common. I'm not going to defend myself in these pages. This will be a record of my journeys throughout the world and my second life as a stone magus. If you're looking for gossip, you won't find it here. And now, since every story must have a beginning, I choose to begin in a village near Kathmandu...

I sat staring at those three little dots for a minute. Deserter? Second life? Stone magus? I already had more questions than I had answers. I found a scrap of paper to mark my place and stripped off my clothes to put on my pajamas. If I were going to deal with multiplying questions, I intended to be comfortable doing it.

It didn't take long for me to forget I was looking for answers. Silas Abernathy had traveled the world, and he'd met so many fascinating people and seen so many incredible things that I soon felt overwhelmed. Unfortunately, his assumption that anyone reading the book would share the same knowledge he had meant he dropped terms like he was scattering seed by the wayside. He referred to stone and steel magi, Neutralities, wards, and the Archmagus without explaining anything about them.

From context, I gathered that stone and steel magi were capable of different magic, and that stone magi like himself could put wards on buildings or nodes that would protect them from the invaders. Mostly. That was what he did in his travels, go from site to site creating or renewing wards. Nothing about why certain sites needed wards or how he did it.

He also mentioned a few other Abernathys, relatives of his, who'd been custodians of the oracular store before him. But he never said why he wasn't a custodian or what it meant that he was a wartime deserter. I checked the front of the book. The publication date was 1957. Presumably that meant World War II. Or—when was the Korean War? I was terrible about historical dates.

After maybe the fifth time he'd casually mentioned another Abernathy, I closed the book and fired up my laptop. But a quick search turned up no Silas Abernathy or any of the other names he'd mentioned. There was no website for the store—well, Mr. Briggs had implied as much. Even so, it felt as if someone had gone out of the way to make Silas Abernathy and the store disappear.

I read about a third of the way through the book before a jaw-cracking yawn made me look at my clock. Just after midnight. And I now had a job to go to in the morning. I set the book aside and turned out the light, then curled up under my blanket. But tired as I was, I couldn't get my thoughts to settle. I stared in the direction of the book, invisible in the darkness, and tried not to remember Mr. Briggs' body, sprawled on the uneven concrete.

I ought to abdicate. This wasn't any of my business. Even without the murder, I was so far in over my head I couldn't even find the surface. I should turn the responsibility over to Judy and walk away. There would be other jobs. Other, less interesting jobs.

How selfish of you to insist on keeping this job just because it's interesting and you're bored. I pulled the pillow from under my head and put it over my face, groaning. What made me think I was the best choice? Well, Silas had somehow seen me, all those years ago—didn't that mean something? And Mr. Briggs wouldn't have hired me if he didn't think I could do the work, and he surely knew best. He'd said I was exactly what he was looking for. Did that mean he'd foreseen me? The idea that the bookstore, not Mr. Briggs, had chosen me made me feel both comforted and inclined to flee.

I could ask the oracle. A simple augury, *Should I abdicate?* A memory sprang to mind, Lucia saying a custodian couldn't use Abernathy's on his or her own behalf, so that wouldn't work. But it wouldn't really be on my behalf, it would be for the sake of the store... or maybe I was reaching for something that would take the decision out of my hands. Even so, it was worth trying. If I could figure out how to do an augury at all.

The air under the pillow was stuffy and smelled strongly of lavender. I put it back and closed my eyes. Another memory, this one more recent —a line from Silas Abernathy's book. *I like to say I didn't choose this path, it chose me,* he wrote, *but that would deny my responsibility for what came of it. And yet I would have been content to stay as I was, had opportunity not presented itself. I can't regret seizing that opportunity, whatever the personal cost.* When I'd read it, I'd been annoyed with Silas for once again being Mister Cryptic. Now it carried new meaning. This was an opportunity I could never have imagined. What would it mean if I turned it down?

It took me another hour to finally fall asleep, but when I did, I'd made my decision.

5

I wasn't surprised to see Malcolm Campbell loitering outside Abernathy's front door the following morning. Even anticipating his presence didn't make me less uneasy about it. "We're not open until ten," I said, hoping to cover my nervousness with an aggressive opening.

"I'll wait," Campbell said. "I hoped you'd let me wait inside."

"I don't know if I should. What about the Accords?"

"You're hardly giving precedence to one side over the other just by letting me in out of the cold." Campbell put the collar of his overcoat up to shield the back of his neck. "You don't even know what side I'm on."

The tip of his nose was red, but that was the only sign the cold had discommoded him at all. Mostly he sounded impatient, the way he had the previous day. "All right," I said, "just don't... don't get in my way." It sounded weak, but Campbell nodded. I unlocked the door and let us both inside.

The smell of onion was stronger today, as if the store had bottled it up against some sort of stink shortage in the future. I waved Campbell in the direction of the metal chair and made my way through the bookcases to the break room. Claiming Mr. Briggs' office, even in so small a way as stowing my purse there, felt awkward. I'd dressed more warmly this day, in a red sweater with a deep cowl neck and black twill pants. Attack of the competent career woman. I'd compromised the look by wearing comfortable shoes, figuring I was likely to be on my feet all day.

Having settled my coat and purse, I crossed the hall to the office. It felt colder than the rest of the building, which was saying something; the rest of the building was only a few degrees warmer than outdoors. *Note to self: find thermostat*. It was probably in the basement, which meant...

I sat in the rolling chair, leaned my elbows on the desk, and buried my face in my hands. I'd have to clean up the bloodstain. I should have worn something scruffy. And I had to mail the catalogues, and Campbell was out there waiting for an augury, and suddenly I wished I knew how to abdicate.

No. I'm not giving up just because it's impossible. I dug some paper out of the filing cabinet, found a pen in the desk drawer, and made a list. It occurred to me that this was a way of putting off the inevitable, namely Campbell's augury, but it was still sensible. I wrote down as many things as I could think of, made a second list of questions I needed answered, and by the time I'd finished both pages I felt calmer, as if I could handle whatever this strange new job required of me.

It was just after ten. I left pen and papers on the desk and returned to the front desk. Campbell was lounging against it, relaxed as a jungle cat ready to pounce. Today's suit was as expensive as the first, and he had his overcoat slung over one arm. "You've had auguries before," I said. Campbell nodded. "Then you can tell me how to do it, because I don't know."

He raised an eyebrow. "I'm not sure how appropriate that is."

"Appropriate or not, Mr. Briggs died before he could pass on any of his wisdom, and I'm not going to ask Judy Rasmussen even though I'm sure she knows."

That made him smile, the faintest tug at his lips. "You've met Miss Rasmussen."

"She was very clear she thought I didn't belong."

"She would be. I'd forgotten she would have expected to inherit the custodianship." He let out a deep breath. "I can only tell you what I've observed. With luck, that will be enough." He pointed at the counter. "There should be a ledger there."

"There is." I retrieved the ledger and opened it to the last page with writing on it. "Do you know what these mean?"

"The name of the person asking for an augury, the date it was given, and the five-digit number is the number of the augury. They're consecutive."

"But I saw Mr. Briggs sell a book without writing anything in the ledger."

"Occasionally ordinary people wander in here and buy things. The books are mundane unless they're selected by the oracle. The custodian. I'm surprised I'm the only one here this morning. Usually Abernathy's is crawling with knowledge seekers. Write my name and today's date."

I wrote everything using my neatest handwriting, which wasn't terribly neat compared to Mr. Briggs'. It wasn't my fault schools didn't teach cursive anymore. "Now what?"

"Now I ask my question, and you find the book that holds the answer. Normally I'd write my question down, but there's only the two of us here, so no worries about privacy."

"How am I supposed to do that?"

Campbell let out his breath in an impatient sigh. "I don't know. That's something only you can work out. Are you ready?"

I didn't think I was ever going to be ready, but I nodded.

Campbell closed his eyes. "What—"

The door opened loudly, startling both of us. Judy Rasmussen, dressed today in a gray coat and matching cap, walked in. She was accompanied by a tall, well-dressed man in his early fifties, with dark hair and round-framed glasses that made him look like a professor of some obscure science. "Campbell," Judy said. "What are you doing here?"

"This is a Neutrality, and I have a right to come for an augury," Campbell said. "I might ask what you're doing here."

"Setting things right. Father, this is Helena Davies. Helena, my father, William Rasmussen."

That was awfully polite. I took Rasmussen's proffered hand, which was firm inside its leather glove. "Pleased to meet you."

"I'm happy to be able to clear this matter up," Rasmussen said. "Did Judy explain how the abdication works?"

"Abdication?" Campbell said.

"No, she didn't, but I—" I said.

"Don't worry. It's painless, and very simple." Rasmussen hadn't let go of my hand. I tried to pull away, but he kept a tight grip. "Just a few words."

"I'm not—"

"I wasn't aware Miss Davies intended to abdicate, Rasmussen," Campbell said coolly.

"She's not obligated to run her every action past you, Campbell," Rasmussen said.

"I don't want—"

"Let her go," Campbell said, putting his hand over our clasped ones.

"Don't touch me," Rasmussen said.

I yanked my hand free. "I am *trying* to say that I'm not going to abdicate."

Rasmussen frowned. "You told Judy you would."

"No, *Judy* said I should abdicate. I thought about it. And I've decided not to."

"You don't know what you're doing," Judy said, "you've had no instruction—it's your obligation to step down."

"I don't think it is," I said. "And if you could learn it, I'm sure I can too."

"Young lady," Rasmussen said, "you're making a big mistake."

"Why, because the oracle won't be under Nicollien control?" Campbell's voice was still cool, but I could hear the triumph in it.

"Are you saying Judy won't be impartial? How dare you make such an accusation?"

"You objected to Serena hosting the last election. Accused her of applying undue influence, and made yourself look like a fool. Are you surprised when the accusation turns on you?"

Rasmussen took a step closer to Campbell. He managed to look menacing despite being an inch or two shorter than Campbell. "Say what you like about me, but no one disparages my daughter—"

"Would both of you shut up!"

My outburst got everyone's attention. "Mr. Rasmussen, I appreciate your willingness to help, but I'm not abdicating the custodianship of Abernathy's. Mr. Campbell, whatever bad blood you have between you, work it out elsewhere. Judy... I like your coat." I took another deep breath. "Now, Mr. Campbell is here for an augury, and I think that should be private, so unless you have other business, I'll have to ask you to excuse us."

Judy's mouth hung open a little, and her black-fringed eyes were wide with astonishment. Rasmussen glared at me, pushed his glasses up higher on his nose, and said, "If you won't see sense, I'll have to take steps to have you removed."

"You can't do that," Campbell said, "and you know it. The Accords are very specific regarding the Neutralities. And I suggest you not threaten a custodian unless you want that getting back to your Archmagus. Which I assure you it will."

Rasmussen spat a nasty profanity at Campbell, then turned on his heel and left the store, Judy following him closely. She glared at me as she left, and I smiled pleasantly at her, though my heart was still hammering from that surge of adrenaline. Where had that come from? I never shouted at strangers—I rarely shouted at anyone.

As soon as the door shut behind them, Campbell said, "Why didn't you abdicate?"

"Not you, too!"

"That was an honest question. You don't know what you're doing, and as far as I can tell, there's no one to teach you."

He did sound curious rather than critical. "Because there must be some reason Mr. Briggs chose me," I said, "and I'm not going to give up without at least trying. If I fail miserably, that's the time to abdicate."

"You realize your failure could be catastrophic to this war," Campbell said. "I ought to insist you stop now."

"You had your chance. Why didn't you?"

"I dislike William Rasmussen too much to give him any sort of victory. I realize that's a personal flaw."

"I take it you're on opposite sides."

"As opposite as you can be. Rasmussen is the local head of the Nicollien faction and I'm a colleague of Serena Parker, head of the Ambrosites. To say we're at odds is an understatement of Biblical proportions."

I leaned back against the counter and felt the ledger shift where I'd laid it on the countertop. "Should we do this augury before anyone else comes in?"

"If you're ready." I was grateful he didn't look dubious, just perfectly composed. "What actions will bring me success in the coming year?"

I waited. "That's it?"

"It's always been enough before." Campbell sighed. "This was a bad idea."

"No, wait. Let me see what I can find." I moved off between the bookcases before he could say anything else that might convince me he was right.

A hush fell over the store before I'd taken more than three steps. It felt like the morning after a heavy snowfall, so rare in Portland—that patient, anticipatory quiet just before someone takes the first step onto a snowy walk, leaving the first footprint. I turned to look back at Campbell, but the bookcases blocked my view. Funny, I hadn't thought I'd gone that far.

I took a few more steps. They were silent, with none of the tapping across the linoleum I'd become familiar with. It should have been unnerving, but it felt peaceful, as if the world was taking a moment to rest and lay down its burdens. I stood still, listening to the rhythm of my breathing.

At the end of the long row of shelves where I stood, one bookcase stood outlined in pale blue light. I drifted in that direction, still feeling utterly relaxed. As I drew closer, I realized the light was coming from behind it, throwing it into contrast like the moon eclipsing the sun. I walked around it to find the source of the light, a glowing book wedged face-down in a pile of tattered children's dictionaries. I hefted the dictionaries out of the way and picked up the book.

The glow immediately faded and then disappeared. The book tingled under my fingers, like gripping a live wire. I examined it carefully. *The Demon-Haunted World*, the spine read, and when I opened the book to the title page, written in silver ink below the title were the words *Malcolm Campbell, $750*. My first augury, and I'd gotten it right.

I closed the book and hugged it to my chest. The tingling spread from my fingers to my body, a surprisingly pleasant carbonated fizz. I made my way back to the front of the store—this took a while, because I'd gotten turned around—and handed Campbell the book. "Seven hundred fifty."

"How do I know this is the right book?" Campbell looked at it dubiously.

"Look inside."

He did so. "I don't see anything unusual."

"Well, let me show you—how did Mr. Briggs prove you had the right augury?"

"I knew and trusted Nathaniel, as annoying as he was. *You* will take some time to adjust to."

I opened the book and pointed at the silver ink. "I don't see anything," Campbell said.

"Well, your name is definitely written there, and the price of the book."

Campbell held the book close to his face. "I doubt you'd dare lie to me."

"Of course not," I said, pretending I hadn't had that thought just minutes before.

Campbell closed the book and reached inside his suit coat. "This should cover it," he said, and held out two glass vials, one larger than the other, both filled with a murky bluish-gray liquid.

"What is it?"

"*Sanguinis sapiens*. Raw magic. It fuels a magus's abilities, and we use it as currency sometimes."

"How do I know it's not colored water?"

Campbell set one vial on the counter and worked free the rubber stopper from the other. "Smell this, but don't breathe too deeply," he said.

I took a delicate sniff. It didn't smell of anything but water and the lingering scent of rubber. "That's hardly evidence—" I began. I glanced at Campbell, then took a longer look. The lines of his face were outlined in glimmering gold, as if someone had traced them with liquid metal. I caught sight of my hand and gasped; it looked the same, only silver-white. A golden light pulsed beneath Campbell's coat like a heartbeat, and his hands and fingernails shone. "Wow," I said.

Campbell smiled. It made his cheek dimple and was the first genuine expression I'd ever seen on his face. "You'll have to trust me that it's enough for the augury," he said, "but then I'm trusting you, so it seems a fair trade."

"All right." I pocketed the vials, one in each pocket—I had an image of them breaking each other, saturating my pants and leg, that I really didn't want to see come true. "Is that... is there anything else I can help you with?"

"I don't think so."

"Maybe... there's something you can help me with?" Campbell raised his eyebrows. "Mr. Briggs... is there magic to, you know, clean up the blood?"

"Lucia didn't take care of that?"

"No."

Campbell swore under his breath. "I'm sorry you were left to deal with it," he said. "Come with me."

The shadows cast by the dangling bulb were deeper today, shifting like something living. I sternly told my imagination to take a back seat and descended the stairs, one hand on the rough unvarnished wood of the rail. My rubber soles made almost no noise on the steps, which creeped me out further. I reached the bottom of the stairs and turned on the light.

Mr. Briggs' blood was a black, dried blotch on the floor. It would take a lot of scrubbing to get it clean. I stood on the bottom step and watched Campbell walk around the bloodstain. "This shouldn't take long," he said, settling his overcoat more securely over one arm. He squatted, and held his hand out palm-down over the dark red smear. The traces of golden light, fading now, gathered from all over his body into his hand.

Campbell clenched his hand into a fist. The golden light coalesced into a ball and fell from his fist to land in the center of the bloodstain. The smell of violets filled the room, and the light spread to fill the space, lapping at the edges of the stain and turning black. Campbell opened his fist, and the black stain began to boil, making small tarry bubbles everywhere it touched the blood. The bubbling increased until the splotch was fizzing like soda poured out on a table. Eventually it stopped. Black flakes covered the place where the blood had been, dry and matte-dull. Campbell stood. "Do you have a broom?"

In one corner there was an industrial-size porcelain sink and a couple of tall, skinny metal lockers. One of them held a broom and a mop. I returned with the broom, and Campbell said, "You can sweep it all up and throw it away. I'd do it, but not in these clothes."

He had a point. "Thanks," I said. I quickly swept the residue into a little pile. There wasn't even a stain to mark where Mr. Briggs had fallen. "I appreciate it."

"Not at all."

Campbell shrugged into his overcoat and followed me upstairs, where he put his hand on the front doorknob. "Miss Davies," he said, "if you're convinced you're the right woman for the job, I suggest you learn quickly. Not everyone who comes looking for an augury will be as accommodating as I."

"You think I can't handle it?"

"I think you need help. Good morning, Miss Davies." He let himself out, and I saw him walk quickly to his Jaguar, head bowed against the intermittent drizzle the wind blew into the glass window. I thought about running after him, insisting that I could handle anything his people threw at me, but that would have been petty and childish. And I didn't want to be either of those things.

6

I went to the office and dug out Campbell's file, then wrote the augury record on the next blank line. I guessed that it was *aug. spec.* like all his others and prayed I wasn't wrong about that. At least now I knew what *sang. sap.* meant. Then I put the file away and sat at Mr. Briggs' desk. My desk, now. Campbell was right; I needed help. I just wasn't sure who to turn to. I remembered my list of questions and swore quietly. He probably knew the answers to some of them, possibly even the most urgent, which was *what is the catalogue for?*

The vials pressed against my legs, hard and cold even through the fabric. Where was I supposed to keep them? I hadn't seen anything like them in my admittedly cursory search of the store. And there was only one other place to look.

Now that Mr. Briggs's presence had been exorcised, I could finally examine the basement. It wasn't as big as the store, maybe half its size, and its low ceiling and exposed beams made it feel claustrophobic. The spaces between the beams were dark, but free from spider webs, for which I was grateful. Cabinets, old-fashioned wooden filing cabinets, lined two of the walls from floor to ceiling. The other two held shelves containing steel safe deposit boxes ranging in size from the width of my hand to the length of my arm. A ring of keys hung from a nail near one of the cabinets. So much for security.

I examined the little keys. Each was stamped with a letter, A through G, and their teeth were worn with use. The boxes were labeled with the same range of letters plus a three-digit number. I tried the C key in box C134; it opened easily. It turned out to be empty. I tried another box and found the key worked there as well. Definitely not the most secure set-up. Had Mr. Briggs' murderer been after the contents of one of these boxes? If so, it seemed unlikely I'd ever find out.

I put the vials of liquid magic into box C134 for lack of any better option. There might be records of the boxes' contents around here somewhere, or their owners. Then I turned my attention to the filing cabinets. My guess was right: they were full of more files like the ones in the office, organized according to the recipient of the augury. And some of them were *old*. I found one dated 1791, the paper crumbling and brown with a dark and dusty scent. I could barely read the name, let alone what book she'd received. The papers weren't as tightly packed as the ones upstairs—there was plenty of room to add more files. I guessed the ones in the office were active files, and these belonged to recipients who were dead. That was a *lot* of auguries over the years.

A couple of drawers held books that turned out to be the cousins of the ledger from the front counter. They were big, heavy, leather-bound tomes filled with lines of crabbed or elegant handwriting, some of it faded with age. I searched the volumes until I found the oldest. *I, Augustus de Kemper, the 14th of May AD 1782*. That was far too old. History wasn't my strong suit, but I was pretty sure there hadn't been any European settlements on this side of the country in 1782 that could support a bookstore. More mysteries to add to my list. But first, I really should try that augury about abdicating.

Far away, I heard the bang of the door opening. I ran up the stairs without turning out the lights and wove my way through the cases to the front of the store. An elderly couple stood there, arm in arm, looking around with interest. The woman turned her attention on me. "You're younger than I expected," she said. "Harry, don't you think she looks young?"

"Can't believe I haven't been in here in ten years," the man said. He was tall and straight-shouldered, with thick white hair cut in a military-style flat top. "Never did care for Briggs. There was something squidgy about him."

"Don't speak ill of the dead, dear."

"I didn't say he was bad, I said squidgy."

"That's not even a word."

"Can I help you?" I said, inserting my words into their conversation like a crowbar. "You can, um, browse if you want—"

"We just came to see you, dear," the woman said. "I'm Harriet Keller. This is my husband Harry. I know, Harry and Harriet, it's funny, isn't it?" She didn't look like she thought it was funny. She looked like someone who was tired of people joking about their names.

"I—" Harriet Keller was much shorter than her husband, gray-haired and plump and wearing a hat that I did think was funny. Not that I would have commented on it. If she'd worn glasses, she would have looked like a stereotypical small-town librarian. "What do you mean, came to see me?"

Harriet smiled, burying her eyes in a mass of wrinkles. "Oh, dear, we're the first, aren't we? With Nathaniel being murdered, and you not being one of us, you'll have to expect a certain amount of curiosity."

"Has this place always smelled of onion?" Harry said, sniffing.

"Harry, be polite."

"That *was* polite. I didn't say 'stink,' did I?" Harry focused on me for the first time since entering. "What's your name, young lady?"

"Helena Davies."

"Funny that it wasn't Judy Rasmussen. I could swear I'd heard she'd be next. Why is that?"

"I don't know. But the store acknowledged me, so I guess it doesn't matter."

"Funny business." Harry shook his head. "Did Nathaniel mail out the catalogues yet? Haven't seen ours. Not to put a burden on you, of course. Hope you don't mind me pointing out you've got quite a job ahead of you."

"The catalogues. I'm mailing those out..." How was I supposed to get all those boxes to the post office? "Soon," I concluded.

"Don't suppose you could give us one? Save you at least a little postage."

"I... yes, I could do that. Wait here, please?" It was irregular, sure, but maybe I could get some information out of these two nice people. Who might only appear to be nice. Wasn't there something about the murderer returning to the scene of the crime? And Harry Keller might be old, but he didn't look like a weakling.

I retrieved a catalogue from the topmost box and brought it back to the Kellers. "I, um, hope you like it," I said, feeling like an idiot. How could I ask them what it was for without betraying how incompetent I was?

Harry and Harriet exchanged a knowing look. "You don't know, do you, dear," Harriet said, putting a wrinkled hand on my arm. "About the catalogue."

I flushed. "No need to be embarrassed," Harry said, "everyone's got to learn somehow." He rolled the catalogue into a cylinder and slapped it once or twice against his palm. "It's a basic divination tool, for the sort of everyday questions that aren't worth paying for a full augury. Wears out after three or four months, but until then—let's show her, shall we?"

Harriet nodded and held out her hand for the catalogue. "Let's see. How about 'where should we eat lunch?'"

"Fair enough." Harriet opened the catalogue and Harry, without looking, planted a long, bony finger in the middle of the page. He glanced down, and scowled. "*Keep the Home Fires Burning.* I wanted to go to IHOP."

"Well, it's not like we're forced to obey," Harriet said, closing the catalogue. "It's only a recommendation."

"So it's... sort of fortune telling?" I said.

"But far more accurate than any horoscope," Harriet said. To my surprise, she reached out and patted my cheek. "Don't worry, dear, you'll do just fine. Nathaniel always swore by that book of his."

"Book?"

Harry and Harriet exchanged glances again. "The custodian's book," Harriet said. "Don't you have it?"

"Oh, *that* book," I said without knowing why I'd lied. "It's... thorough."

"See? Harry, we really should come in for an augury soon." Harriet linked her arm with her husband's again. "Good luck, dear."

I leaned against the countertop after they'd left and let my eyes focus on the knob for lack of anything better to do. So there was a book, one I hadn't found yet, and it presumably had everything I needed to know. Why had I lied? *Because I don't want people knowing how lost I am.* I turned around and went back to the office. The augury could wait. A more thorough search was in order. I was going to find that book if it took all day.

The door banged open again. I ran back in time to see a man in a heavy coat and a mail carrier's uniform drop a bundle of letters and shiny mailers on the counter. "Have a nice day," he said. I picked through the letters once he was gone. None of them had return addresses. All of them were typical white business-sized envelopes that didn't feel like they had more than one sheet of paper inside. I tore one open and shook out the contents.

There was no salutation, just a single handwritten line: *Is my mother trying to kill me?* Then, below, a name and address somewhere in New Orleans. I stared at it. All right, so people could mail in their questions for auguries. Presumably I'd have to ship them the books. And bill them. I dropped the letter on the counter and massaged the bridge of my nose. Like I needed more impossible tasks. I gathered up the mail and took it back to Mr. Briggs' office. These could wait until I found the book.

But it turned out Harriet had been wrong about people's interest in me. There was a *lot* of curiosity. Five minutes after the Kellers left, another customer—the kind who knew what Abernathy's was—came through the door. Then another. By noon, the place was... not crowded exactly, but after the quiet and emptiness of the previous day, it felt packed to overflowing. Most of them, again as predicted by Harriet, only wanted to meet me. After the tenth introduction, I gave up on trying to remember their names.

Three of them wanted to buy auguries. They didn't seem to mind the audience, but I asked them to write their questions down anyway. I gave my best impression of someone who knew what she was doing and accepted payment—two fat unmarked envelopes and a stack of musty books with cracked leather bindings. I shoved the last at random onto one of the shelves, reasoning if Abernathy's worked the way Lucia had explained, organizing the new acquisitions was the last thing I should do. I hoped the books were valuable enough to cover the augury they paid for.

The second augury gave me a clue as to the mysterious *aug. fam.* notation. The woman, a tall Amazon named Bethany, said, "It's on behalf of my brother, not personal," as she handed me a slip of paper with her question written on it. I nodded like that made sense. Presumably Abernathy's knew what kind of augury to produce even if I didn't. Personal augury, family augury maybe, and *aug. spec.*—another thing I could have asked Campbell. But I was learning.

I carved out some time around two o'clock to shovel reheated lasagna into my complaining stomach. People kept showing up and prowling the shelves, just as if this were any ordinary bookstore. After lunch, I sold a couple of books the mundane way to a bright-eyed man wearing an outdated fedora—at least, I thought it was a fedora, Viv always complained people got those confused with trilbys, and it was certainly a mystery to me. "I promise this isn't a cheap way to get around paying for an augury," he said with a wink.

"I know," I said, though I'd been wondering. "I'm surprised anyone ever finds anything worth reading in here. It seems unlikely."

"You never know where an interesting book will turn up." He accepted the two books from me; they'd turned out to have prices written in pencil inside the front cover. "I'm Ross Dunlop, by the way. Nathaniel was a good friend of mine."

"Oh! I'm sorry for your loss."

"Thanks. It's... I hope you don't take this the wrong way, but it's hard seeing you behind the counter."

I wasn't sure what to say to that. "I'm sorry."

"It's a real tragedy. This store was his life. He must have seen something remarkable in you, to turn it over to you."

Our other criteria won't matter to you, Mr. Briggs had said. For the first time since his death, I wondered what he'd meant. I also wondered why I hadn't spoken to more grieving friends. Or relatives—

"Did Mr. Briggs have family?" I asked.

"No. He never married, and he was an only child." Dunlop straightened his hat. "Good luck to you. I'm sure that custodian's book is a real blessing."

I nodded and closed the cash register, making its bell chime. Apparently, I was the only person who didn't know about the custodian's book. My search of the office, cut short by the arrival of more customers, hadn't turned anything up. It was probably somewhere in the basement.

I glanced up as the door opened again, smiling to cover my frustration. I would have to come in early tomorrow morning, or stay late tonight, and I still hadn't addressed the catalogues. How had Mr. Briggs managed without an assistant? Though, granted, he probably hadn't been as popular as the mysterious new custodian seemed to be.

I did one more augury before six o'clock. I felt more confident than I had with Campbell waiting by the front door that morning. By then, the hordes of people had mostly dwindled away, and I was able to take the final augury payment—a tube of *sanguinis sapiens* and an envelope full of twenties—to the basement.

I put the tube into C134 with the others, then stepped back to regard the room. Where would Mr. Briggs have put something as important as an instruction manual for an oracular bookstore? That was probably the wrong question. He knew enough about the store not to need to consult the manual for every little thing. So it wasn't likely to be somewhere obvious and accessible.

Distantly, I heard the door open and close. I checked my phone—just after six o'clock. Hadn't I locked the front door? I trudged up the stairs, wishing my feet didn't ache so much. Last customer, then I'd search the basement for real.

There was no one waiting by the front door when I arrived. I cursed silently, then called out, "I'm sorry, but I have to close up now. You can come back tomorrow."

No answer. No movement. The lights seemed faded, insufficient illumination now that the sun had set. I rubbed my arms against the sudden chill in the air and headed toward the office, cursing silently. I hadn't heard the door again, so unless someone had just stuck their head in and changed their mind about entering, that person was still in the store. "Hello?"

I came around a corner and had to stifle a shriek, because I'd nearly run into someone. She was tall and thin, with a sort of pale elven beauty, and without thinking I checked her ears. Well, *I* didn't know if elves were real. I was willing to believe pretty much anything at that point. But she seemed as human as me, if more fashion-model-like. She was dressed entirely in white, down to the long parka trimmed with, I was certain, real ermine. Her pale lips, frost-kissed, drew up into a silent O of surprise, but otherwise she didn't react to my sudden appearance.

"Can I help you with something?" I said. "Only we're closed now."

"I don't need anything from the store." She adjusted the silver-shot white scarf around her neck, and light reflected off her ring, the biggest diamond I'd ever seen outside fashion magazines. "It's something Mr. Briggs was holding for me. I'd like it back."

"Um... sure. What was it?"

"Some papers. I'm sure they're in the office. I'll show you which ones."

"I haven't seen any papers that weren't to do with Abernathy's. But I can look again."

The woman in white followed me to the office and stood, watching, while I checked all the drawers of the desk and the filing cabinet.

"Maybe he kept it filed with your augury records," I finally said. "What's your name?"

"Eisen. Georgina Eisen. But I don't—that is, go ahead and look." She'd twisted her scarf entirely around her hand now, and her eyes darted restlessly from me to the cabinet to the photos on the walls as if she were assessing the possibility that they might attack her.

"Can you spell that for me?"

"E-I-S-E-N."

I dug through the records. There was a Stephen Eisen, but no Georgina. "I'm sorry, I don't know where else to look."

The hand tightened on the scarf. "They must be there. It's important. You just overlooked them."

I closed the drawer, slowly. "If they're here, I'll find them eventually. I don't have time to search now. Why don't you come back tomorrow?"

"But I need them now."

I could suddenly see this conversation stretching out into the wee hours of the night. "I don't know what you want me to do. If you tell me what papers to look for, I'll set them aside for you—"

"Never mind. I'll come back later." She was gone before I could finish my sentence, the heels of her white boots flashing at me as she left the office at a near-run. I followed her, heard the door open and shut, and emerged from the bookcases to find myself the only one in Abernathy's. Finally.

I locked the door and put up the sign, then retreated to the basement stairs, but as I passed the office, I had an idea. It was sort of cheesy, but I *had* looked everywhere else.

In the office, I lifted the framed photo of the bald hat-wearing man off the wall. Bingo. A wall safe, one old enough to be original to this building, stared back at me. My satisfaction at guessing right faded as I realized I had no way of opening the thing. I put the photo back and stared at it. "You could be more helpful," I told the man in the photo. He didn't answer.

I took a sheet of paper from the filing cabinet and scribbled a few questions until I found one I liked: *Will Abernathy's be better off if*

Helena Davies abdicates? I tore off the others and folded the augury request in half, then walked back to the bookcases and took a few tentative steps in. By this time, I was familiar with the silent, timeless feeling of the oracle around me, but the feeling didn't arise. I took a few more steps. I felt nothing but the chill of the store, heard only the distant sound of traffic and my feet tapping across the linoleum. I wandered through the bookcases for a few minutes, but it was obvious the oracle declined to answer. I felt relieved and disappointed all at once. Maybe I wasn't meant to work here, but the oracle wasn't going to give me an easy out.

I managed to search half the file cabinet drawers in the basement before I had to call it quits and run for the bus. I didn't have enough *time*. And Campbell was right; I needed help. Not that I knew who to ask. Judy Rasmussen... probably a bad idea, and she didn't like me very much anyway. Malcolm Campbell no doubt had his own concerns. None of the customers I'd met that day struck me as knowing any more about Abernathy's than I did. That left Lucia, and I didn't know how to reach her.

I leaned my head back against the bus window, which was frigid thanks to the coming snowstorm. I might not know how to reach Lucia, but somebody did. I just had to ask around tomorrow. Anyone who commanded the obedience of bruisers who could manhandle a body into a van would know *someone* who could crack a safe.

My pocket chimed a relaxing tinkle of bells. I pulled it out. "Viv?"

"Sweetie! Why are you not answering my texts?"

I flicked through the displays. Ten in a row. "I've been busy. I didn't even notice them."

"You work too hard. We're going out tonight. No arguments. Also, I'm getting rid of this oatmeal-colored thing in your closet. It doesn't suit you. I'm not sure who it would suit. One of those mopey Communist hausfraus, probably."

"Viv, are you in my *room?*"

"I'm buying you nail polish next time we go out. And eyeliner. Wow, Hel, where did you *get* this dress? The bargain rack at Sears?"

"That's rich, coming from the woman who only shops thrift stores."

"I have nothing against Sears except all their clothes look the same. So do yours. How does your boss expect you to dress for work? Career casual, or your usual jeans and sweater ensemble?"

I gently banged my head against the freezing window. Sometimes I had trouble remembering why Viv and I, so very different, were friends. "Don't throw my clothes out, Viv."

"I make no promises. Hurry up! The boys will be waiting."

"Boys?"

7

O'Hara's wasn't an Irish pub, despite the name. The large windows glowed golden against the backdrop of a frozen evening, warm and welcoming. I hurried to follow Viv through the door and a mass of muggy air struck me, enveloping me in its embrace. It might be uncomfortably warm later, but for now it felt wonderful. I shed my unfashionable coat and ran my fingers through my hair to straighten out the tangles. The smell of craft beers filled the air, tempered by a whiff of sweetness, the perfume of the woman standing next to the door. I smiled at her as I passed, a friendly acknowledgement that we both existed, and she smiled absently back. It felt like an omen of good things to come.

Up-tempo bluegrass fusion music played in the background, just loud enough that the conversations going on around me were pitched to carry across the pub. It wasn't very crowded for a Friday night, though I was sure things would pick up once the seven o'clock movie showings let out and people arrived for a nightcap.

Viv found us a table next to the wall, not too near the bar. I leaned against its artfully exposed brickwork and felt my chair shift as its uneven legs tipped me back. I was so glad to be sitting down, I didn't feel like moving. Even the tangerine stiletto heels Viv had forced me to wear couldn't ruin my mood, though my toes were verging on numb.

It always surprised me how comfortable I felt in the outfits Viv selected for me. Not physically comfortable—the shoes always pinched—but emotionally so. I'd never have her fashion sense, and she didn't try to dress me like herself, but I looked... maybe not glamorous, but groomed, at least. She'd matched my favorite jeans with a sweater I'd forgotten I had and insisted I wear the heels instead of my comfortable boots. With my hair brushed out and the dreaded eyeliner applied, I looked chic. Not as chic as Viv, in her multicolored bohemian tunic and red velvet leggings, but enough that I didn't feel out of place surrounded by the young and hip who frequented O'Hara's.

"They're supposed to meet us at eight," Viv said, picking at a chip on the edge of the table with a turquoise-enameled fingernail. "Then we're going for dinner. Then back here for more booze." She wore her hair shaved close to her scalp on one side and in a flip that reached her chin on the other. This week, it was dyed a bright magenta that looked more pink under the bar's low lighting.

"Who are these guys, anyway?"

"I met Shawn at my last gig. He was *very* appreciative of a female drummer." Viv's lips curved in a reminiscent smile. "I haven't met his friend, but Shawn says he's funny and smart, so I figured he sounded like your type."

"You thought *Chet* was my type."

"And he was, for about two weeks. It's not my fault you have trouble breaking a man's heart." Viv half-rose from her seat. "That's Shawn, and... ooh, he's cute!"

I had no idea which of the two men approaching us was destined to be my date, but they were both cute. One of them was beefier, with longish black hair, and the other was thin and tall with brown hair and an artfully unshaven face. Viv hopped up and kissed the beefy one on the cheek. "Shawn, this is my friend Helena. Helena, this is Shawn and... is it Brian?"

"It is," the tall one said, nodding at me. "Can I get you something to drink, Helena?"

"Something pale, thanks."

"And I already know you like it dark and strong," Shawn said, putting his arm around Viv's waist. She laughed and pushed him in the direction of the bar.

"See? He's *really* cute," Viv said, using her hand to shield her mouth, not that anyone could have heard her in that din.

"I'll give you cute, but he might have an awful personality," I said.

"Oh, don't be so pessimistic. He's got good manners, what else do you want?"

"Someone smart enough not to bang his head on the table to knock a few words loose."

"Chet only did that once."

"Once was more than enough."

"Would you stop talking about your ex while you're on a date with someone else? It's like you're still in love with him."

"I was never in love with Chet. Infatuated, maybe. And I'm going to stop talking about him now." I never thought about Chet unless I was on a date, and then it was only to be grateful we weren't together anymore. He'd been my first serious boyfriend, and we'd been together for eight months, six of which I'd spent wishing I knew how to blow him off. I glanced toward the bar where Brian and Shawn stood chatting and waiting for their drinks. Brian was cute, and unless he turned out to be a serial killer or political science major, he had potential.

I smiled at him when he returned, glasses in hand, and offered me something straw-pale that tasted wonderful. "Thanks."

"No problem. So, are you in school?"

"No, I work at a bookstore."

"That sounds like a dream job. If you're a reader, that is. You look like a reader."

I had no idea what to say to that. "It's never dull."

"Helena started yesterday, and it beats working at the Pick 'n'

Pack," Viv said. She was snuggled up next to Shawn and sipping her stout. "Beats my job, that's for sure."

"Waitresses keep society moving," Shawn intoned, making Viv giggle. "Seriously, what would we do without the service industry? That's why I always tip well. They get no appreciation."

"What if the service sucks?" Brian said. "Should you still tip?"

"Sure, why not? You don't know what they've been going through. Maybe they just got a divorce or something."

"*I* appreciate it when people tip," Viv said.

"I always think of you when I tip," I said. "What do you do, Brian? Are you in school?"

"I'm studying to be a teacher. History."

"Speaking of underappreciated professions," Viv said.

Brian smiled. "I believe in following your dreams. I've always wanted to teach high school. Had a really great teacher my senior year, Mrs. Costas, and she sort of inspired me."

"I think that's great," I said. "I wish I knew what I wanted to do. I've never felt inspired by anything." I remembered Silas Abernathy's book, and how connected I'd felt to the store, and wondered if that were still true.

"Give it time," Brian said. "You don't strike me as someone who meanders through life."

I smiled and took another drink. He was cute, and nice, and he wanted to be a teacher, and if his casual flirting was a little obvious, at least he was interested.

We chatted for another fifteen minutes, enough for me to finish my drink and establish that Brian liked professional baseball, superhero movies, and crème brûlée. He was also funny in an understated way and capable of talking about his interests so even I, who didn't care for organized sports and preferred classic films, was able to appreciate them. By the time we pushed back our chairs and headed for the door, I was enjoying myself and silently thanking Viv for having good taste in men.

The air smelled crisp and cold, promising a clear night, and I filled my lungs with it, reflecting how much nicer cold air was when it didn't smell of onion. Brian and I trailed Viv and Shawn, who walked with their arms linked and occasionally kissed as they went. "How long has she known Shawn?" Brian asked.

"A week, maybe?" I wasn't actually sure about that, but Viv could go from zero to sixty in about two seconds when it came to men. "She knows what she wants and she's not afraid to go after it."

Brian shoved his hands deeper into his coat pockets. "I know she's swept him off his feet. I hope she isn't setting him up for disappointment."

"Viv's always sincere when she's attracted to someone. She doesn't toy with men."

"I didn't mean it that way. It's just that he's been burned before, and I'd hate to see it happen again."

I couldn't think of a response that wouldn't be defensive and angry. So Viv was quick to display her emotions. That didn't make her a slut, or whatever Brian was implying. "They're both adults. They know what they're doing."

"Yeah, I guess." Brian stopped. "What's that?"

We were passing a narrow, dark alley between a couple of red-brick buildings. "What?"

"It sounded like a dog. An injured dog." Brian took a few steps into the alley.

"You should leave it alone. An injured dog could be dangerous."

"I'm good with animals. Can't you hear it?"

I did hear it now, a high-pitched whimper that sobbed out for a few seconds, then stilled. Brian took another step. The whimper started again. "Brian, I really don't think this is a good idea."

Brian ignored me. "Come here, boy," he murmured, and whistled between his teeth.

Against my better judgment, I followed Brian, staying several paces behind him. "Seriously, what are you going to do if it comes to you? We can't take it with us." Red light pulsed at the end of the alley, shed by a neon sign on the hotel across the way. It cast Brian's features in hellish relief. I stepped around a crushed cardboard box labeled THIS END UP and shied away from something that moved behind it. A rat. "Let's go. We can call Animal Control and get them to pick it up."

A pile of wooden crates stacked haphazardly to chest height looked as if it might come down at any second. Brian crouched in front of it. "I see you," he said, and held out his hand. "Come on, boy, let me help—"

The crates exploded upward. Something big and black that gleamed sickeningly in the neon glow reared up, taller than Brian, taller than the second-story windows. Tentacles lashed out, wrapping Brian's arms to his side, whipping around his throat and mouth. He lurched once, then the tentacles lifted him off his feet, thrashing with his desperate attempts to get free.

I screamed. It was impossible to move; I was rooted to the ground as surely as if I'd been bound by those tentacles too. Instantly the thing's attention was on me. I saw no eyes, no head, but I knew it was watching me. It dropped Brian, who hit the cracked asphalt with a terrible loose-limbed thump. Then the tentacles stretched out toward me, feeling their way as if the thing truly were blind. I screamed again and finally, *finally* turned to run.

Black-clad figures pounded into the alley, streaming past me, jostling me as they ran. I turned around again, stunned, and saw them taking up positions between me and the tentacled thing. One of them raised a fat-barreled gun to his shoulder and fired what looked like a beanbag. It expanded into a fine mesh that covered the thing in a spider's web of paint or white ink. The whimpering broke out again, only this time it was loud and piercing, the cry of something in terrible pain.

Another of the figures stepped forward, extending a hand toward the thing palm-out as if in warning. A tentacle lashed out, wrapping itself around his wrist. "Don't let it touch you!" I shouted, stupidly.

The man ignored me. Steel flashed, and the now-severed tentacle fell away in two pieces. The man brought his knife around again and slashed at the thing's center, the place where all the tentacles emerged. More tentacles lashed at him, but as quickly as they gripped him the knife severed them. It was like a fatal dance, and even as stunned as I was, part of me was impressed.

Hands gripped my shoulders and spun me around. "You can see us," the man said. His face was nearly as dark as his clothing, and he was only a few inches taller than me. I tried to wrench myself from his grasp, but he held me with no more difficulty than a man restraining a kitten.

"Who are you? What *is* that thing?"

The man looked past me. "We have a problem," he said.

I craned my head around to see the man with the knife sheathe his blade and kneel next to a pile of black, dismembered creature parts. "Not now," he said, and I recognized the voice of Malcolm Campbell.

I gasped. "What—"

"Hel, where did you go?" Viv called out. My eyes met those of the man restraining me.

"Quincy," Campbell said, and a black-clad woman moved to the mouth of the alley. I saw her unroll a strip of paper she had looped around her wrist. I opened my mouth to call out to Viv and a firm hand went over my mouth. I tried again to get away from him, fighting with every ounce of strength I possessed, but it was useless.

The woman shook the paper out a few times. It snapped in the cold air, cracking like a whip. Swiftly she slapped it against the nearest wall, smoothing it out. It stuck there as if glued. She laid her palm over it, and a flash of white light filled that end of the alley, then vanished. A second later, Viv and Shawn walked past, moving quickly and looking in all directions. "Helena?" Viv called out. Her voice was slightly muffled, as if she'd pulled her scarf over her face. Then they were gone.

My captor's grip loosened, though not enough for me to free myself. "What the *hell* was that all about?" I shouted.

"Miss Davies," Campbell said. He sounded surprised. "What are you doing here?"

"I was on a date, and Brian—" The air suddenly felt much colder. "Is he all right?"

"He's dead," Campbell said.

His words came to me echoing, from far away. "Dead?"

"You can let her go, Tinsley."

I yanked myself free of my captor and turned to face Campbell. He had a welt across one cheekbone and his dark hair was mussed, and the same irrelevant part of me thought, *He looks even better that way*. "He can't be dead," I said.

"Encounters with invaders are nearly always fatal, especially for the non-magical." He extended a hand to me. "I'm sorry for your loss. Were you close?"

I shook my head. "I only met him half an hour ago, but..." I took Campbell's hand and let him draw me closer to where Brian lay, his body limp and his limbs tangled as if he'd fallen from a great height, dropped by some giant hand. His eyes were wide open in astonishment, and his mouth was blackened, like he'd eaten a lot of licorice. The comparison was too much, and I turned and vomited into the scattered crates. My throat and mouth burned with alcohol-tinged bile.

Campbell helped me to my feet when I finished. I was shaking everywhere. "That was one of the invaders," I said.

"I'm glad you're not the fainting type," Campbell said. "Yes, and our illusions will wear off soon, so we have to act quickly."

"We have to call 9-1-1," I said, then felt stupid. "But how will they explain his body? It looks like he died of fright."

"That's not too far off the mark. It's not a pleasant death." Campbell nodded at Quincy, who still had her hand on the strip of paper. "Illusion holding steady?"

"Five minutes."

Campbell turned back to me. "I'm going to have to ask for your help," he said.

"She's a civilian," the man with the unusual gun said.

"This is Abernathy's new custodian. She's one of us, more or less." Campbell squeezed my hand, then released me. "You and the young man were mugged. He took your purse—here, give it to me. Don't worry, I'll make sure it's returned to you. Your date fought back and the mugger shot him, then ran away. Stick to that story, don't embellish it, and you'll be fine."

I nodded. The cold had made me so numb I couldn't feel anything, not surprise or horror or even fear. "But he's not shot."

Campbell drew a pistol from a holster strapped to his thigh. "He will be." He nodded at Quincy. "You have that illusion ready?"

Quincy closed her eyes and let out a long breath. The air beside her quivered, thickening like heat haze. Heat would have been welcome just then. I didn't see anything else, but after a minute Campbell said, "Take a good look at him. You'll need to be able to describe him."

"I don't see anything but a sort of haze in the air."

Campbell gave me an intense, narrow-eyed look. "Strange. And you saw through our concealment. I'll have to investigate that later. Very well. Your attacker was white, with dark hair and a scruffy beard. He wore a black knit cap and a trench coat. That's all you remember."

I repeated the details back to him. "Miss Davies, I'm truly sorry you were mixed up in this," Campbell said. He pointed the gun at Brian's body, then squeezed off two shots. The explosive sound echoed in the alley, and I involuntarily covered my ears and closed my eyes. When I opened them, Campbell's people were gone, and blood was trickling from two bullet wounds in Brian's chest.

That's impossible, he's already dead, his heart isn't beating. I threw myself to my knees beside him. Campbell was wrong, Brian was still alive. He'd just shot a helpless man in the chest. For the second time in as many days I put my cheek to a dead man's mouth, hoping to feel air sighing out. Nothing. I couldn't understand how Brian could still be bleeding. I stripped off my coat and pressed it hard against his chest. "Help me!" I shouted. "Somebody help!"

Running footsteps sounded behind me. "Helena, what happened?" Viv came to a stop next to me. "Are you all right?"

"Mugger—call 9-1-1—he's bleeding." My breath was ragged as if I'd been running, and the cold air felt like a knife in my chest. I heard Shawn talking to someone, sounded like a 9-1-1 call, but it was so distant. Brian's slack face, his... how odd, his mouth wasn't black anymore... it all seemed impossible. Unreal. Two days ago I'd been a total innocent, and now this mysterious war had reached out and touched me. Had killed someone I knew, however slightly. He'd wanted to be a teacher and now he was dead. I felt as if I should be crying, but my dry eyes ached from the numbness that filled me.

Viv was saying something I couldn't understand. I shook my head with no idea whether that was an appropriate response. "It was a mugger," I said. "He took my purse, Brian stood up to him, and he shot him. Shot Brian."

Then there were sirens, and paramedics, and police officers. Someone took the coat out of my hands and moved me to stand by the wall. How long would they try to revive him? Wasn't it obvious he was dead? I realized I had a blanket wrapped around my shoulders. I didn't remember taking it, but I huddled more closely into it. The noise, and the flashing lights, and the unrelenting cold had turned the whole thing into a nightmare, something I would surely wake from soon. I found myself remembering Campbell's grip on my hand—his hand, that he'd then used to shoot Brian's body. How many times had he seen this happen, that he could be so callous about it? I shivered, then couldn't stop shaking.

"Miss, could you step this way, please?"

It was the police detective who'd arrived with her partner shortly after the uniformed cops had showed up to throw a barrier around the crime scene. I obediently followed her deeper into the alley, past where the tentacled horror—the invader—had attacked Brian. There was no sign of its dismembered body now.

"I'm Detective Sutherland," the woman said. She had dark skin and dark hair in hundreds of tiny braids bundled up at the base of her neck. "Can you tell me what happened?"

I repeated Campbell's story for her, resisting the urge to embellish. Detective Sutherland had a patient air about her, one that begged you to fill up the silence with more details. When I finished, she said, "Which way did the murderer run?"

"Out the front of the alley. I didn't see which way he turned."

"And Mr. Valley challenged him? Refused to give up his wallet?"

It took me a moment to realize Mr. Valley was Brian. "Are you saying it's his fault he got shot?"

"I'm just trying to establish the facts, Miss Davies." The slam of the ambulance door snapped me out of my stupor. I blinked at Sutherland, but she was writing something in a small brown notebook. "The fault is entirely the killer's. You handed over your purse immediately?"

"It didn't have anything in it worth dying over. Some money, my credit card and driver's license."

"We'll search the area. Usually they dump what they can't use. Did the killer say anything else?"

"Like what?"

"Any other threats. Anything to say he'd targeted the two of you on purpose."

"Nothing like that."

Sutherland closed her notebook with a snap. "We may have more questions for you later, but right now I think you should go home. You look like you're in shock."

I picked my way past the crime scene investigators, going over the alley for forensic evidence. What would they make of what they found? Would the medical examiner find evidence that Brian was already dead when he was shot? I shivered again. What time was it? I realized my phone had been in my purse and hoped Campbell would return that too.

"Helena, you look awful." Viv wrapped her arms around me and hugged me tight. "Can you go home? They don't want you to go to the station or anything?"

"She said they'd have more questions later. Viv, let's just go."

The ride in Viv's ancient Econoline van was unexpectedly quiet. Normally the thing rattled and clunked loudly enough to drown out the noise of Viv's drum kit, which was packed tightly in blankets but whose cases bumped the walls at every pothole. I curled into a ball on the passenger seat and stared sightlessly out the window. Brian was dead. I couldn't stop seeing his look of utter surprise when the thing grabbed him, and how empty that look had been when he lay on the ground with two bullet holes in his chest. The numbness had passed, leaving me cold and achy all over.

"You could have died," Viv said. "Helena, it could have been you."

"I know," I said. "I don't know what to feel right now. Poor Brian."

"Shawn went to the hospital behind the ambulance, even though he... anyway, he wanted to be there when Brian's parents arrived. It all happened so quickly, you know? We didn't realize you weren't with us, and then—I swear, Helena, we passed that alley and didn't see anything. It was weird."

"We were... pretty far back." The crates, exploding outward as the thing reared up from its hiding place—the stench of my vomit, puddling nearby—Brian's dead face—I started shaking again, and this time tears leaked from my eyes.

"Don't cry, sweetie, don't cry—it's going to be all right."

I shook my head and wiped away tears. "I know. It's not like I even knew him, right? But he was right there next to me, and..." I didn't know how to finish that sentence. What would have happened if Brian hadn't followed the "dog" into the alley? It finally occurred to me to wonder what Campbell's group was doing there. Chasing after the invader? I wished I knew how to contact him. I had so many more questions than I'd had even this morning.

The house was dark when Viv pulled into my parents' driveway. "Do you want me to come in with you?"

"I'll be fine. Thanks."

"Call me in the morning, okay? I'm not kidding. If you don't, I'll show up at your store and make a fuss until you prove you're all right."

Her swoop of hair obscured one eye, but what I could see of her face was serious. "I'll call."

Viv waited until I had the front door open before driving away. I went to take off my coat and realized the paramedics, or someone, still had it, and I was still wrapped in the scratchy gray blanket. Well, it was ruined, wherever it was.

I bundled the blanket in my arms and tiptoed to the stairs. Music and muffled conversation floated up the stairwell, telling me that at least one of my parents was still up, watching TV. There was no way to my bedroom except past the sectional and television, but I didn't want to talk about my ordeal... except if I didn't, I'd get an earful in the morning. I made my way down the stairs, trying not to think about Brian's parents and the conversation they were no doubt having now.

8

I slept poorly, convinced there was an invader hiding in the shadows, waking just enough to feel paralyzed. When my alarm finally went off, I smacked the snooze button with the palm of my hand and lay staring at the ceiling. Its rough texture made curving lines I was long familiar with; I'd made pictures out of them since I was a kid. The sailing ship. The daisy in profile. The skull—I shuddered and looked away. I didn't need any reminders of death.

Jake was already gone when I went upstairs, but Mom had made chocolate chip pancakes with marionberry jam, and she stacked my plate high with them. Her sympathy made me irritable, which made me feel guilty. She was only trying to help. I just didn't want to feel like a victim when I wasn't the one who'd died.

I had to wear my dress coat to work, which made me even more irritable, because it was a long black quilted thing with faux fur trim that made my face itch if I put the hood up. It made me look like I was going to a funeral. More reminders of death. Should I go to Brian's funeral? What was the etiquette for the death of someone you barely knew who'd died right next to you? It was the kind of thing Viv would know.

The bus ride felt longer than normal, the streets rougher than usual, something I noticed because I had to ride standing up due to crowding. Clinging to the hand loop, I stared at the back of the person next to me. He wore a dark blue denim jacket and workman's boots. He was probably going to some job where he'd build things, or dig things up—something practical, anyway. Whereas I would fumble around inside a smelly bookstore, completely at a loss and pretending I knew what I was doing. My third day on the job and I was still no closer to competence than when I'd walked in two days ago.

It was nearly ten when I let myself in Abernathy's front door. No one was waiting outside, for which I was grateful. I put my coat and purse in the office and picked up the list I'd made the day before. Wonderful. Not only couldn't I mark anything off, I had to add things to the list, like getting into the wall safe. I scribbled a few notes to myself, then stood leaning against the desk, closed my eyes, and breathed in and out rhythmically for a minute. I'd committed to this job and I was damn well going to do it. And the first thing I would do today was start addressing those catalogues. It was a little thing, but it was under my control.

I left the office door open while I removed catalogues from boxes and applied the labels, then put them back into the boxes. Then I had to take them out again to apply postage, which came out of a special machine on the edge of the desk. I hoped it was set to the right amount.

I'd gone through one box and most of a second when I heard the door slam. I ran to the front and found Campbell loitering near the cash register. "Oh," I said, "it's you." Gone was the black-clad gun-wielding man of the previous night. Campbell was once again dressed in an expensive suit and tie, his gold watch glinting at the edge of his left cuff. The welt had vanished. I felt a moment's disappointment, though he looked almost as good as he had in the black fatigues.

He smiled slightly. "I suppose it makes sense you wouldn't be thrilled to see me. How are you?"

"Fine. Still shaken. And full of questions."

"They can wait." He extended a phone toward me. It looked like the phone he'd taken from me the night before, but black instead of white. "You put in a claim for a lost phone this morning and paid for a replacement. This phone already has your old number assigned to it. You also called your bank and credit card company to cancel your cards. Replacements are in the mail. The police will have found your purse and driver's license early this morning and should call to let you know about it soon." He handed me a wad of bills. "This is the cash that was in your wallet. Sorry about the inconvenience."

"How did you manage all that?"

"I have connections."

"Because you're a magus?"

"Because I run a company that handles these things all the time. Diantha even looks a little like you. Any other questions?"

I couldn't think where to start. "How do I contact Lucia?"

He raised an eyebrow. "That's not what I thought you'd ask."

"It's the simplest question I can deal with right now."

He held out his hand. "I'll put her number into your phone. That's the trouble with mobiles these days—no more little black books other people can pry into. Otherwise you'd have all Nathaniel's contacts already."

"Aren't you a little young to be complaining about the good old days?"

He smiled again. "You'll notice I'm not giving up my phone in protest." He handed my new one back to me. "Now. About last night."

"What *was* that thing? How did it find us?"

"That was, as I think I told you, an invader. One of the small ones."

"That was *small?*"

"The big ones, the ones that find a way in where they aren't noticed and stopped immediately, can be the size of a city block. Have you ever read H. P. Lovecraft?"

"No."

"You probably should. He saw these things more clearly than anyone ever has, and he wrote about them, though he dressed it up in terms of his imaginary mythos to protect the magical community. At any rate, his descriptions are accurate."

"But Brian didn't see it. He said he saw a dog, just before... the end."

"They're good at illusion. They weave it the way a spider spins a web, then wait for someone to fall into it."

"Then why could I see the truth?"

"I don't know. Possibly it's part of being Abernathy's custodian. Nathaniel never mentioned it, but many custodians have abilities bestowed on them by virtue of their positions. Seeing things as they are would fit your job description, as it were. You certainly had to be altered to use the oracle."

I leaned against the countertop and crossed my arms over my chest. I didn't like the sound of "altered." "Those things can't be common, or we'd hear about all these mysterious deaths."

"They're not as uncommon as we'd like. Mostly they prey on the weak—sick people, the old and the very young—and the deaths they cause look natural, at least enough that a casual investigation won't prove otherwise. The one you met in that alley was either stupid or desperate to set up its lure there."

"Because no one would believe someone Brian's age died of a heart attack."

"Precisely. I'm sorry I had to shoot him, but he and you would have come in for much different scrutiny otherwise."

"And you made an illusion of the shooter fleeing as part of the deception."

"Quincy did, yes. I'm not skilled enough in illusion—that's a paper magus's specialty."

"I don't—there are different kinds of magi, right? Stone magus, steel magus, paper magus... what else?"

"Wood, stone, steel, bone, paper, glass." Campbell ticked them off on his fingers. "I'm—"

His suit coat made a chiming noise, and Campbell pressed his hand flat against his chest. "Sorry, I've got an appointment. Call

Lucia. She can answer most of your questions. She should have done that already."

"She said she didn't know anything about Abernathy's."

"There's a lot about the magical world that doesn't have anything to do with this store."

"Wait." I took a few steps toward him as if that would keep him there. "I've lived my whole life in this city and never saw one of these invaders. Then suddenly I'm dropped into this... magical world... and right away someone I know is killed by one? Isn't that a huge coincidence?"

Campbell shook his head. "You want to know the truth?" he said. "The one last night wasn't there at random. For an invader to be off on its own like that... it was pursuing strong sources of magic, and as Abernathy's custodian, that now includes you."

For a moment, the shadows shifted, and I saw tentacles in every corner. "I'm... what?"

"You give off traces of the magic that makes Abernathy's work."

"That sounds... eerie. Like I've started glowing in the dark."

"Nothing so dramatic. Even most magi won't be able to tell. But invaders definitely will."

"Will I be attacked?"

"They don't usually go after the strong and healthy. And this store is strongly warded against them. Invaders getting their teeth into a Neutrality... that's one of my nightmares. Don't worry about it." He nodded at me, then left before I could say anything else.

I stared after him for a few seconds, realized I was shaking, and had to lean against the counter until my hands stopped trembling. It was all very well for Campbell to tell me not to worry—he probably killed three invaders every morning before breakfast just to stay loose. I, on the other hand, had no defense other than the ability to see through their illusions. I wished Campbell would come back so I could yell at him, or punch him in the face, or something to make myself feel better. But at this point there was nothing I could do except keep a careful watch on the shadows.

I took out my phone and called the number he'd given me. It rang several times without picking up, then went to voice mail. "It's Helena Davies," I said. "I need help getting into a safe in the office and I figured you'd know someone who could do that. Thanks."

The door opened as I hung up. "Good, you're alone," Judy Rasmussen said. "I thought we should talk." She was in her Jackie Kennedy getup again, wearing a jaunty cap over her dark hair and a pair of black boots I instantly envied. At least I didn't feel so rumpled as I had the first time she'd entered the store.

"If you're going to try to convince me to abdicate, you can forget it," I said.

"Do you know about the upcoming augury?"

"The... is someone on their way?"

"It's more than that. Serena Parker is stepping down as local head of the Ambrosites and the Ambrosite Archmagus is coming here for an augury in a few days to determine who should take her place."

"But Abernathy's won't answer any questions starting with 'who'."

"You wouldn't understand the details. But it's a big deal. And you don't know anything about it."

"Then tell me. Or are you going to be spiteful about this?"

"It's not something I can explain. Please, see sense. Abernathy's is going to fall apart unless you abdicate."

"I'm doing all right so far."

"'All right' isn't exactly a ringing endorsement." Judy unbuttoned her coat, revealing a short gray jumper over a white blouse. "I've been trained to do this for twelve years—"

"If that's the case, why didn't Mr. Briggs hire you?"

Judy's lips thinned. "I don't know."

"The store accepted me. I'm the custodian. Look, you know I could use some help. Why can't you work with me?"

Judy shook her head. Without another word, she turned and left the store, letting the door slam shut behind her. I watched her through the windows as she walked away, and sighed. Well, if I'd been in Judy's position I doubt I'd have wanted to help me either.

I went back to the office to work on the catalogues, but was interrupted by more customers, all of whom wanted to get a look at me. I did my best to stay polite, but I felt like a sideshow freak. Some of them wanted auguries I could tell they'd made up to give themselves an excuse to come in. I collected their payments and made another mental note—*Depositing cash, where and how?*

By noon my cheeks were stiff from polite smiling. The pile of addressed and stamped catalogues was slowly growing. I sat behind the cash register on the rickety metal stool and ran my fingers over the worn keys while I waited for the newest "customer" to get bored and leave. I had Mom's pad thai waiting for me in the break room and my stomach was starting to send messages that it was interested in making its acquaintance.

The door flew open. "A safe, huh?" Lucia said. She was accompanied by the same blond bruisers I'd seen take Mr. Briggs' body away. "You," she added, pointing at the middle-aged man who'd been pretending to browse the shelves, "out."

"Thanks for coming," I said to the man, who scurried away. "You could have been more polite," I told Lucia, but secretly I was grateful for her forcefulness. "I didn't expect you to come in person."

"I'm more than a little curious about what Briggs had stashed away. Where is it?"

I led the little procession to the office and took the picture off the wall. "Henry, Maxwell, get to it," Lucia said.

One of the men opened a small black satchel and removed the strangest stethoscope I'd ever seen. The tubing and earpieces were normal, but the part you put against someone's chest was clear glass. Maxwell (or Henry) fitted the earpieces to his ears and pressed the glass bell against the safe door, close to the dial. His partner removed one of those rubber reflex testing hammers from the bag and tapped it against the door.

A tone like the lowest note on a xylophone filled the room. The man with the stethoscope spun the dial rapidly counterclockwise. "Thirteen," he said, and waited. It took me a second to realize he'd been addressing me. I scrambled to find paper and a pen and wrote thirteen at the top. The man with the hammer tapped the door again, and his partner spun the wheel, clockwise this time. "Twenty-two."

They repeated the steps once more, and the man said, "Five." He stepped away from the safe and put the stethoscope back in the bag. "That's left, right, left," he told me.

I nodded and stepped to the safe. Thirteen left, twenty-two right, five left. The safe clicked open. "Thanks," I said.

"Go ahead and examine the basement," Lucia said, and the two men left the room.

"Excuse me? Nobody's allowed to roam the store without my permission."

"It's part of the murder investigation, Davies, don't get your panties in a twist. And I don't want the boys in here for this. It's possible Briggs stored things in here that people shouldn't know about."

"What about you knowing about them?"

Lucia gave me a disdainful look. "Just empty it out, Davies."

The safe was deeper than it was tall, and full of all sorts of things, mostly manila envelopes with metal clasps. I piled them on the desk and Lucia started sorting through them. "Anything interesting?"

"Not yet—holy hell," Lucia said. I turned in time to see her pull out an eight-by-ten glossy photo of a couple of people on a bed, very naked and very intimate with one another. "That's Mark Curtin."

"Should I know him?"

"He's a powerful stone magus. And that woman is definitely not his wife." Lucia opened another envelope. "This is documentation... it's an affidavit swearing that Sariah Monk bribed someone to gain her place on the Nicollien Council. More photos...this is all blackmail material."

"A woman came in yesterday looking for papers she said Mr. Briggs was holding for her. She got very nervous when I couldn't find them. He had to have been blackmailing her."

"This is a *lot* of evidence." Lucia shoved some photos into their envelope and dropped it onto the pile. "Suddenly Briggs being murdered makes sense."

"You think one of his victims got fed up?"

"It's possible. We're still trying to work out the details. We know the murder was committed with an ordinary knife, not magic. Briggs wasn't expecting it—he wasn't fleeing his attacker. And now we know that someone, a lot of someones, had reason to want him dead."

I shuffled through the envelopes until I found one labeled EISEN. "What should I do with all this? I certainly don't want to blackmail anyone!"

"I'll take it. I need to know who had a motive for murder. Now, what else is in there?"

There were a few vials of *sanguinis sapiens*, a jeweler's box containing a diamond necklace that made me gasp, and an old pocket watch stopped at 9:52. No books. I sighed. "Not satisfied with the necklace?" Lucia said.

I almost told her about the missing instruction manual, but decided against making myself look even less competent than I was sure I already did. "Looking for something that will tell me what's in those safe deposit boxes, or who they belong to, or something like that."

"There's a master list somewhere of the owners. I've seen it because I signed for one myself. It's the best security there is."

"I think the fact that anyone could walk in and take the key off the wall says it isn't."

Lucia favored me with her disdainful look again. "Come with me."

We went down to the basement, where Maxwell and Henry were busy examining the walls above the filing cabinets, feeling the rough concrete surfaces as if searching for secret doors. One of them pressed the tip of his nose to the wall and sniffed deeply, his eyes closed. Lucia seemed not to think this was odd. "Henry, hand me those keys."

Henry—he was slightly shorter than Maxwell, and had a prominent chin—stopped what he was doing and turned to face Lucia. "*Those* keys?"

"Did I stutter?"

Henry glanced at me, then back at Lucia. "I'm not stupid."

"No, you're not." Lucia walked over to the keys, licked her finger, then gingerly brushed its damp tip across one of the keys.

Electrical energy zapped a blue-white arc from the keys to Lucia's finger, and the woman staggered backward into Maxwell. He supported her as she sagged, breathing heavily, cradling her finger to her chest. "That's just a light touch. Try to hold one, and you'd better hope your will is up to date."

"It didn't do that to me... and I suppose only the custodian can handle them safely."

"You got it, Davies." Lucia pushed herself upright and patted Maxwell's arm in thanks. "Did you find anything?"

"Traces of two people," Maxwell said. His voice was deep and pleasant to match his face and I found I liked him. Not that I knew anything about him other than his ability to crack a safe. "A conversation, then Briggs turns away and the second man stabs him in the back."

"Then you know it's a man."

"Maybe seventy percent certain. A man or a tall woman, definitely."

"How do you know?" I asked.

"Glass magi have the gift of perception," Lucia said. "They can see traces of magic, see the imprints people leave on the space around them. You didn't see where the attacker went?"

"It took skill to see him, or her, at all. But there's nothing that says the attacker didn't take the stairs."

"And yet he didn't attack you," Lucia mused. "What else—oh." She went to the farthest cabinet and reached into the bottom drawer. "This is the register," she said, handing me a long, skinny notebook bound in brown leather. I opened it to see a list of alphanumeric entries that matched the number-letter combinations on the safe deposit boxes. Next to most of them were names, though some of those names had been crossed out and new names written beside them. Not all the boxes were currently rented, though I already knew this, but a good portion of them were.

There was a sheet of paper tucked into a pocket inside the front cover. It was a typewritten list of prices, A through G, and it only took me a few seconds to realize they were the rental rates. Finally something was going my way, though no one who'd entered the store had been interested in renting a box so far. I closed the binder and thanked Lucia, who waved it away.

"Thank me when this augury is over," she said.

"When is it supposed to happen?" I was proud of how casual I sounded, like I was already competent and everything.

"Next week. Six days from now, anyway. I hope you're ready."

"It doesn't sound like a very common occurrence. Why is Ms. Parker stepping down?"

"She's accepted a position with the Ambrosite Archmagus's organization. It's very prestigious." Lucia snorted. "Sounds like more work to me, but I'm not a magus and no one's asking me to take on the job."

"Is there a favorite? Or do they really depend on the oracle to choose the new head?"

"There's always private wagering, but yes, it's all up to the augury. I'm sure a lot of people would like it to be Campbell, though nobody would hate it more than him."

"He fights the invaders. Like some kind of commando."

Lucia laughed. "He was a Navy SEAL once. Don't let the suit fool you."

That explained how he could move like a greased cat. "Why the suit, then?"

"He owns a private security firm catering to the very wealthy. Has to look respectable to sell his services. But he's a stone-cold killer when it suits him."

Campbell hadn't struck me as particularly stone cold, but then I hardly knew the man. Even so, the idea made me uncomfortable. The way he'd so casually put two bullets into Brian's dead body... "You make him sound like an action hero—rich, handsome, influential, ex-military. Does he also have a tragic past?"

"His father was killed in action four years ago, very unexpectedly, which is when Campbell took up the family business. He doesn't talk about it."

I'd been kidding, and now I felt guilty at being so flippant. "I don't want to pry."

"Then stop asking questions," Lucia said, but she was smiling like it wasn't a reproof. "Maxwell, Henry, if you're done, we should get back. Unless you have any other questions?"

"No—yes. Can I use your van to get these catalogues to the post office?"

"Why don't you take Briggs' car?" Lucia dug in her pocket and came up with two keys and a fob on a simple steel ring. "It's old, but he took care of it like it was his baby. I'm sure it's big enough for you to haul your load. Gray Honda Civic, and it's parked in the lot behind the building. I doubt it's been towed."

9

I thanked her and her "boys," then put up the CLOSED sign, locked the front door and hurried around the block to the rear of the store. It was a bright, sunny day, but that wasn't enough to dispel the chill in the air. Exhaust fumes wrinkled my nose as a pickup pulling a loaded, tarp-covered trailer drove ponderously past. I hadn't paid much attention to the neighborhood when I arrived that first day, and I'd been too busy to pay any attention to it after that, but now I looked around, curious about Abernathy's neighbors.

Most of the buildings on the other side of the street were newer than Abernathy's. In fact, Abernathy's and whatever lay above it were probably the oldest structures on the street. A market with small windows was on its immediate right, reminding me that I still hadn't eaten. To the left, big black letters proclaimed that this was the Barden Theater, and handbills and posters decorated its windows. I'd never heard of the advertised movie, but I thought I might stop in some evening, just for fun.

The parking lot, marked PRIVATE, was nestled deep within the surrounding buildings, which were tall enough to prevent any sunlight from reaching the ground. It looked cold and felt colder. I saw a narrow alley slit off one side and guessed it was the one that hard-to-open door led to. Not that I had any interest in traveling that route, which was filthy and claustrophobic.

I searched around until I found a gray Civic parked near the exit. Frost crystals still ringed the front and rear windows, but it didn't look like sitting out in the cold for two nights had hurt it at all. I unlocked it, then stood shivering with my hand on the door. As bad as taking over Mr. Briggs' office had been, this felt a hundred times worse, going through a dead man's car. I wondered once again if anyone outside the magical community would miss him. What a lonely life, if he hadn't even had a sister or lover or children.

I opened the door and looked inside. Mr. Briggs had kept his car spotless; there wasn't a cheeseburger wrapper or loose penny to be seen. I hesitated again, then opened the glove box. Owner's manual for a 2008 Honda Civic EX, proof of registration, a folded map of Portland. Nothing personal at all. I worked the seat latch to push the passenger seat all the way forward, then stepped back. There would be barely enough room for me to shove all those boxes into the back seat and fit a few up front.

I got in the driver's seat and had to adjust it forward so I could reach the pedals, though not far—Mr. Briggs hadn't been much taller than me. The car smelled of pine from the air freshener attached to the air vent, and I breathed in and tried not to feel as if I were driving a stolen vehicle. *That parking spot in front of the store had better still be open.*

The parking spot wasn't open. A familiar Econoline van was using it. Viv, wearing a neon orange vest with fake leopard fur trim and a maroon peasant skirt, stood on tiptoes peering through the store window. I parked across the street and hurried over. "You took my spot."

"It didn't have your name on it. What is your store doing closing in the middle of the day? Suppose I had a book-related emergency?"

I unlocked the door and ushered her in. "You'd have to go elsewhere. Seriously, Viv, what are you doing here? Don't you have work?"

"I only work half days on Saturday. Wow, this place smells like onion." Viv sniffed ostentatiously. "It looks old. Shouldn't your boss, I don't know, set up some displays or something? People aren't going to want to buy anything from a place that looks this."

"I just sell the books," I lied. "You want to look around? I have to move stuff. Or you could help." Frankly, hauling the boxes in Viv's van would be tons easier than using the Civic.

"Help how?"

I gave Viv a quick tour of the premises. Viv looked at the stack of cartons with a skeptical eye. "You're not going to make it to the post office in time."

"Why not?"

"Weekend, remember? It closes at two."

"Great. No, I forgot."

"We'll put them in the van anyway, and I can drop them off Monday morning. Your boss sure has you doing the grunt work, doesn't he?"

You have no idea. "I'll probably work my way up the food chain. Let's get these loaded."

It felt so much faster having someone help with the lifting. I paused as I put the final carton into the van and looked across the street at Mr. Briggs' car. I should probably move it back to the parking lot, in case someone objected to its being parked at the curb for hours, but I was tired and sweating and decided I didn't care all that much.

When I returned to the store, Viv had disappeared. I called her name and got no response. I checked the office and discovered the door to the stairs was ajar. "Viv?"

"Just poking around," she called out, and seconds later she emerged from the back stairs. "Wondering what's up there."

"I don't know. I don't have the key."

"Storerooms? Or does your boss live up there? Lots of these older buildings have apartments above."

"I... don't think so. I've never seen him go up there." *Perfectly true.*

"Want me to break in? I can do it."

"Viv!"

She patted her vest over her left breast. "I've even got my picks."

"That's *illegal*, Viv."

"It's only illegal if they catch you with them in a place you're not supposed to be."

"I don't think that's true. And this would qualify."

"Hey, I'm just offering you options."

"If I want to know, I'll ask my boss." I'd forgotten about Viv's latest project, lock picking, and I wished I'd come up with a reason to have her unlock the mysterious door. I hadn't thought much about it, what with everything else that had preoccupied me, but I was curious about what was behind it. *Now* it occurred to me that I could have had Maxwell or Henry unlock it, if I'd thought about it at all. Too late now.

Viv followed me into the break room and sat at the table while I heated up the pad thai. "You want some?"

"I ate already. I'll just steal a few bites." That, in Viv-speak, meant she'd eat at least half of what I had. I sat down opposite her and dug in, half-listening for the sound of the front door opening. "So where is your boss?" Viv continued. "You're not on your own, are you?"

"He'll be back soon. Just went to run a few errands." I hoped Viv hadn't seen me pull up in a car that didn't belong to me and start asking questions about those nonexistent errands.

"At least it's an easy job. Not a lot of customers, I'd imagine."

At that moment, the door opened and closed with a familiar *bang*. I sighed and pushed my meal in Viv's direction. "I'd better go see what they need."

Two men in trench coats stood inside the door. One of them, a tall, thin man with olive skin and dark hair, was scanning the shelves, his nose slightly wrinkled as if he didn't like the smell of onion. I could hardly blame him. The other, short and blond, was flipping through the stack of remaindered books on the counter.

"Can I help you with something?" I said.

The man turned his attention from the shelves to me. "Detective

Acosta," he said, displaying his badge. "This is Detective Green. We're here about the murder of Nathaniel Briggs."

The room swam, and I grabbed hold of the counter to keep from falling over. "Murder?"

"Can you tell me where you were two nights ago between the hours of five and seven, miss?"

Time blurred together in my memory. So much had happened... "I was here until six o'clock. Then I rode the bus home. I live with my family. Mr. Briggs was murdered?" How could they possibly have found out? Didn't Lucia still have the body? And why between five and seven? He'd been killed sometime around noon.

"Nathaniel Briggs' body was found early this morning. We're trying to trace his movements before that. You were in this store all day Thursday?"

"No—yes—I was hired Thursday morning."

"By the victim?"

"Yes."

The detective took out a little notebook, like they did in TV shows. His partner moved off into the store. I tried to keep an eye on him, but he soon disappeared between the shelves. "Can you describe the victim's movements on Thursday?"

Great. Would this guy be able to tell I was lying? *Keep it simple.* "He hired me around ten-thirty and put me to work typing labels. Around noon he came in and said he had to go out for a while, it might be a long while, and that I should lock up if he wasn't back by six. He wasn't. So I locked the store and went home. The next morning, he wasn't here when I arrived, so I opened the store and went on with my work."

"Didn't you think it was strange that he'd leave you, a brand-new employee, to run the store without assistance?"

I shrugged. "He told me when he hired me that he wanted employees to show initiative."

"And this morning, when he once again didn't arrive?"

I couldn't make this situation sound less strange than it was. "He'd said that sometimes he had to go on buying trips for a day or two and he didn't want me overreacting if he did. But I was going to call the police tomorrow morning if he wasn't back. I figured that was long enough. I didn't want to raise a fuss too soon and then find out it was all perfectly normal."

"Hmm." The detective put his notebook away. "This is an odd store. Get many customers?"

"A few."

The door opened, and Ross Dunlop entered. "I'm sorry, is this a bad time?" he said.

"No, please look around." I willed Dunlop to hear my real meaning—*don't do anything stupid*—and turned my attention back to Detective Acosta. "Is there anything else you want to know?"

"Your name and address, please."

I gave it to him and he wrote it down. "I'll be in touch if we have any more questions, but you should probably not leave town."

"Am I a suspect?" I could hear someone, either Detective Green or Dunlop, moving around in the shelves; the sound echoed strangely off the ceiling, whispering words I couldn't understand.

"You may have more information to give us," Acosta said, which struck me as more ominous than if he'd just said yes. "Good afternoon, Miss Davies." He nodded at Green, who'd emerged noiselessly from the shelves, and the two of them left.

I held onto the counter hard, trying for the third time in as many days to calm my shaking. "Miss Davies?" I heard Dunlop say, distantly. "Were they investigating the murder?"

"I have to call Lucia," I said, struggling to get my phone out of my pocket. It had gone in crooked and my trembling fingers couldn't hold onto it. "She should have warned me."

"Sit down and relax," Dunlop said, guiding me to the folding chair. "It's all right. You stayed calm, and they won't suspect you."

"But they had the time of death wrong—they shouldn't have found his body, right? Shouldn't Lucia have kept it hidden, or disposed of it more permanently?"

"I don't know." Dunlop crouched in front of me and rubbed my clenched hands. "Don't panic. Just take a deep breath, yes, like that.

Now let it out." I breathed as instructed. "You do that for a minute. I'm going to check the wards."

"What does that mean?"

Dunlop patted my hand. "I'm a stone magus. We can set up resonances in stone that... we think of it as canceling out an invader's frequency, though that's no more accurate than saying they come from a parallel dimension. At any rate, the wards prevent invaders from passing through to consume magic or attack people. Abernathy's is full of magic, so its wards are essential. It occurred to me that someone could have sneaked through the foundations to attack Nathaniel if the wards were weak, so I came to examine them. If that's all right."

"Yes, please do." I sat in the freezing chair and waited until my shivering was from cold and not nerves. Part of me wanted to watch Dunlop, see what kind of magic went into wards, but I was afraid I might fall over if I tried to stand. Eventually I felt sturdy enough to go back to the office. No, the break room. Maybe Viv had left me some food.

Viv. I'd forgotten she was there. What was she doing?

I found her in the office, lounging in the rolling chair. "Sorry about that," I said. "Did you hear any of it?"

"Of course. I was practically duty-bound to listen. It's not every day someone gets involved in a murder investigation. No, wait, for you it *is* every day." She was making a chain of paper clips, one end of which was hooked through her ear.

"I know. Weird, huh?"

"What's weird is you told me your boss had left this morning to run errands. As in, you'd seen and spoken to him today. Not something you told the police."

Words failed me. "You must have misunderstood me. I just said he was running errands. I didn't want anyone to worry that he'd left me to handle all this myself."

"So when you told that other man you didn't know how they could have found out about the murder, and why hadn't someone disposed of the body more securely, that was also something you didn't want me to worry about? Helena, what are you mixed up in?"

"I'm not—"

"You're one of the worst liars in the world, you know that, right? At least I've never had trouble knowing when you're lying. You have a tell."

"I do not. What is it?"

"What, and have you stop doing it and lose my edge? Come on, Helena, tell me the truth. This is two murders in two days. If you're involved with the Mob, I think I have a right to know."

She was leaning forward, drumming her fingertips on the desk-top, and the paperclip string dangling from her earlobe wasn't as comical as I'd expected. I stared her down, wondering what my tell was. No one had said I couldn't tell anyone what I'd learned; that had been implied, that no one would believe the story, that people would think I was crazy and maybe even lock me up.

But this was Viv, who'd known me practically my whole life and kept all my secrets, even the ones she got in trouble for. If anyone was going to believe me, it would be her. And I found I desperately wanted to tell *someone* what had happened to turn my life inside out.

"You're going to think I'm crazy," I said, "but remember I've never lied to you except that one time, and that was for a surprise party."

"I live for crazy," Viv said. "Tell me."

So I did. Everything from when I walked into Abernathy's, to being hired, to discovering Mr. Briggs' body and the things Campbell and Lucia had told me. When I finished, Viv's eyes were narrowed in thought. She carefully unhooked the paperclips from her ear and said, "Do you have superpowers?"

"I don't think so, except maybe being able to see through illu-sions. The auguries are all the store's. I'm just its hands."

"That is too damn cool for words." Viv strolled over to the filing cabinet and looked at one of the folders. "Codes, magic, predicting the future… of course you couldn't give this up."

"I'm not so sure, half the time. There's so much I don't know."

"It sounds like dead Mr. Briggs chose you for a reason. Though I have to say, it's suspicious."

"What is?"

"It's almost like he chose you for your ignorance. Are you sure he didn't predict his death?"

"Lucia said we can't use Abernathy's for our personal benefit. So I'm reasonably sure."

"Then that means he expected to go on living and he wanted you to follow orders. You wouldn't know enough to ask the right questions. Or the inconvenient ones."

"He did say I didn't have any bad habits to unlearn."

Someone knocked on the office door. "I'm done," Dunlop said, poking his head inside. "Everything looks fine."

"Thanks, Mr. Dunlop."

"No problem. And let me know if you learn anything about Nathaniel's murder? I want the bastard brought to justice." He nodded, then withdrew.

"You were going to call someone," Viv prodded.

"Right." I dialed Lucia's number. Once again, the call went to voice mail. It wouldn't surprise me to learn she did that on purpose. I summarized the visit I'd had and asked her to call back. "I hope I don't get into trouble for telling you all that."

"What are they going to do, fire you?" Viv said. "Though I wonder why they keep it all a secret. You'd think the more people knew about these invaders, the safer everyone would be. People would know what to be cautious of, for one."

"Or people would panic and open themselves to greater danger."

"That's possible." The front door banged open. "Does it always make that much noise?"

"It's like a warning system. I think bells would sound nicer. But that's so far down my to-do list I can't even see it."

Viv followed me out into the store, where I found Harry and Harriet Keller once again standing arm in arm, examining the cash register. "It's quite the period piece, isn't it, dear?" Harriet said.

"I can't believe it still works," I agreed. "Can I help you with something?"

"We wanted to invite you for supper tonight," Harriet said. "A sort of welcome to the neighborhood, as it were."

"Nothing formal, just a few friends," Harry said.

"Thanks, I... that would be nice."

Harriet beamed at me and patted my arm. "Who's this?"

"My friend Viv. Viv, this is Harry and Harriet Keller." Viv grinned. I elbowed her as discreetly as I could manage. "Let me write down your address."

"Give me your number, and I'll text it to you," Harry said. "Or did you think us old folks were too out of touch with modern technology?"

"Not at all," I lied, and recited my number. Harry swiftly entered it, and a few seconds later my phone buzzed with an incoming text.

"Seven o'clock, and don't worry about bringing anything," Harriet said. "Have a nice day, dear. It was lovely to meet you, Viv."

When the door closed behind them, Viv burst out, "Harry and Harriet?"

"Shut up. They're nice and it's hardly their fault what their names are."

"And they're—what did you call them, magi?"

"I think so. There seem to be a lot of people who know the secret who aren't magi. Like Lucia. And me."

"Well," said Viv, "you can add me to that number."

MR. BRIGGS' car drove like a dream, for something that had almost 120,000 miles on it. I checked my rearview mirror every five seconds, looking for cop cars. It was possible the car had some kind of warrant out on it—could cars have warrants?—or at least something that associated it with a murder investigation. But I didn't have any other way to get to the Kellers', and I didn't like telling them no just because I was afraid of the slim chance I'd get pulled over.

Rain had started falling about an hour before closing, a freezing rain just this side of slushy, and it had reduced the number of customers to zero. Viv left around that time, promising to come to my house Sunday for some kind of fun that would let both of us forget about our jobs. I locked up around 6:30 and headed through the busy streets toward Arlington Heights.

The Kellers lived in an upscale neighborhood, nestled into the gentle hills west of town. I skidded occasionally going up the rain-slick roads and tried not to think about how I was going to get back. Most of the houses were the sort of blocky, modernist construction I admired without wanting to live in one. Not that anyone was asking me to. I was fairly certain the Kellers were as wealthy as Malcolm Campbell, in their own idiosyncratic way.

I slowed to a crawl, looking for the Kellers' driveway. Trees clung to the curbs and the steep hills where the houses perched, obscuring their lower levels. Lights from the windows gilded the tops of the trees, but cast the streets into shadow. I drove past a hedge, registered the house number was the one I was looking for, and backed up to make a turn into a curving driveway that circled the house. Dead-headed rosebushes brushed the car windows as I passed. The driveway would be beautiful in summer.

The Kellers' house was gray, trimmed in either dark gray or blue; I couldn't tell in the darkness. A BMW was parked in the driveway—not the sort of vehicle I'd pictured them driving. I pulled into the driveway next to it and sat for a few seconds with the ignition turned off. I'd already decided it would be bad manners to bring a list of questions to a dinner party, demanding answers, but friendly conversation couldn't be wrong. Friendly conversation that happened to touch on some of the many, many things I wanted to know was perfectly acceptable. I ran over a few of those questions in my head, things like *What do different kinds of magi do?* and *Who was Silas Abernathy?* Though I wasn't sure it would be polite to ask the latter, if his reputation was as dire as he'd implied.

The rain was turning to sleet. I hurried from the car to the front door and knocked, huddling into my coat. There was a garden gnome in the planter next to the front porch, its rosy cheeks and bright eyes gleaming at me in the porch light. I hoped it meant the Kellers had a whimsical sense of humor, and wasn't a sign of tacky bad taste.

The door opened. "Oh, good, you're here," Harriet said. "Come in, dear, it's so nasty outside. I hope you didn't have any trouble getting up the hill. Some years we're completely iced in—though that never lasts long, right?" She winked, leaving me confused as to what she meant. I handed her my coat and followed her into a spacious sitting room.

"Good to—" Harry said.

I screamed. Scrabbling along the carpet toward me was a chitinous thing, with too many legs and an oversized head. Dripping mandibles gnashed in my direction. Its eyes, deep red like drops of blood, swiveled on eye stalks, looking everywhere at once. I screamed again and bolted for the door.

10

"Wait!" Harriet said, grabbing my shoulders with a surprisingly firm grip. I tore free with some effort and had my hand on the knob when she said, "Oh, dear, we should have warned you about our familiar."

The door was locked. She'd locked it. I fumbled at the deadbolt, turning it—no, now I'd locked myself in. Harriet put her hand on mine. "I had no idea you could see its true form. Calm down, dear, it can't hurt anyone."

I turned around and pressed my back to the door as if I could force my way through. "That... *thing*... why—"

"It's perfectly safe," Harry said. He rose from his recliner, tugging on a long chain leash to bring the thing in check, and bent to pat it between its eye stalks. Its fangs dripped sticky goo that boiled in the air and evaporated before it hit the carpet. "I'll take it outside if that will make you more comfortable. Will?"

I realized Harry wasn't the only one in the room. William Rasmussen rose from the pale gray sofa where he'd been sitting next to Judy. On a nearby loveseat sat a woman I didn't know, her spiky red hair a stark contrast to her pale surroundings. She took up all the space on the loveseat, with her muscular arms stretched out across its back and her long legs extended in front of her, as relaxed as if nothing were wrong.

Another creature perched on her lap, this one a vivid green and segmented like a caterpillar, but with razor-sharp teeth in a circle where a head should be. I heard a high-pitched whine that felt as if it were coming from inside my head, and released the breath I'd been holding. Now I could see the evil caterpillar had a strange sort of harness strapped around its midsection, all silver metal and black webbing, attached to a chain leash. So did the eyestalk creature, and a third monster I hadn't registered because I'd been so freaked out. The third monster looked like it had been flayed; its "skin" was red and glistening, with thick blue veins spidering across its surface. A faint smell of paint thinner wafted from their direction.

All three of the monsters were straining at their leashes, trying to reach me. Rasmussen pulled hard on the leash of the flayed one, forcing it away. "Brittany, leash it in the sun porch," Harry said, and the leggy redhead stood, slowly, an act of defiance, though Harry didn't seem put out by it.

I stayed pressed against the door until all three creatures had disappeared down the hall. "You think those are under control?" I said, my voice shaking. Forget the leashes—those things would have torn me apart given an opportunity.

"How can you see them?" Judy said. "Those are permanent illusions."

"I'm the custodian of Abernathy's," I said, and couldn't stop myself giving her a smug look. Judy's eyes narrowed. Well, I was feeling rattled.

"Sit down, dear, and let me get you some wine, you look like you need it," Harriet said, steering me to a second recliner. I perched on its edge and looked around. The Kellers were as enamored of pale colors as the outside of their house suggested; all the furniture was white or pale gray, the deep pile of the carpet was a gray a few shades darker than the recliner, and the drinks cupboard was a light ash rubbed to a silvery sheen. An odd coffee table that looked more like a giant prism framed in ash lay at the center of the seating arrangement. Landscapes hung on the walls, the only colors in the entire room. A fire burned in the fireplace, behind brass andirons that caught the reflections of the flames and made the hearth glow. It reminded me of something you'd find in a home decorating magazine, cold despite the fire.

Harriet handed me a glass of pale wine. Of course she wouldn't serve anything here that might stain if it spilled. "I really am sorry," she said. "That must have been a terrible shock."

"First exposure to familiars, eh?" Harry said, taking his seat. Rasmussen and the woman he'd called Brittany followed suit. I covertly examined her. She reminded me of Campbell, all that coiled tension ready to leap into action. But where Campbell had that air of being permanently annoyed with the world, Brittany gave off a sense of self-possession, as if she knew she was good at whatever it was she did and was proud of herself. She made me nervous.

Rasmussen, on the other hand, examined me openly. "So you can see through those illusions," he said. "Is that an advantage, or not?"

"What are those things supposed to look like? They smell awful."

"Dogs," Brittany said. "Big ones. The kind you'd expect to maul a child, given the opportunity. You get used to the smell."

"Why do you—how can you keep them under control?"

"Why? Because their magic can attack their kind directly," Rasmussen said. "A familiar lets someone who isn't a steel or wood magus go into combat with the invaders. It expands our pool of fighters substantially. As to how, well, that's the harness—and the smell is a side effect. I'd explain the ritual that binds a familiar, but it wouldn't mean anything to you."

He didn't sound disdainful. He sounded polite, friendly even, and I was having trouble reconciling this man with the one who'd been so angry when I wouldn't abdicate. "If this is a ploy to get me to change my mind—"

"I wouldn't abuse our hosts' hospitality that way." Rasmussen accepted a glass of the pale wine from Harriet. "The Kellers thought you'd like to get to know some of our people outside work, so to speak."

"Where are my manners?" Harry said. "Helena, it seems you've already met Will Rasmussen. This is his daughter Judy, and Brittany Spinelli. She's a steel magus and a damn fine one. What do you mean, change your mind?"

I decided not to start a fight in the Kellers' living room. "It's nothing. Thank you for inviting me."

"Supper's ready," Harriet said, "if you'd all join me in the dining room?"

The dining table, made of glossy red oak, was big enough to seat twelve. Harriet had set the table so we all clustered at one end, companionably. I tried not to feel nervous about the fine china place settings or the many forks. I did know how to behave myself in a formal dining situation, but it left me on edge nevertheless. A cut-glass chandelier hovered over the center of the table, reflected brilliantly on the table's surface, and I wondered why there was no tablecloth. I put my napkin in my lap and wished I were dressed appropriately, though no one else wore formal attire. Rasmussen, in his suit with pocket square, came the closest to looking dressed-up.

"Helena," Harry said, "tell us a little about yourself. What brought you to Abernathy's?"

It reminded me of dinner at Chet's house, months ago, the time I met his parents. They'd grilled me on my education, and my family, and my prospects, until I'd nearly forgotten my own name. "I, um, answered an ad in the paper—"

Judy made an indelicate noise. She was seated directly opposite me, and I saw her cheeks go even rosier. I ignored her. "Mr. Briggs told me I was exactly what he was looking for, and he hired me. If he hadn't been murdered"—*is murder a polite topic of conversation at dinner?*—"who knows how long I might have gone without knowing any of this existed?"

"You must feel terribly overwhelmed," Harriet said. Coming from her, it was an expression of sympathy and not a thinly-veiled jab.

"A little, but I'm learning fast." I took a large bite of green salad to give myself an excuse not to speak for a moment.

"You haven't told your family, have you?" Brittany said. She made it sound as if telling people was the worst sin she could imagine.

"No. I don't think they'd believe me." I didn't mention Viv. That was none of their business. "Pardon me if this is stupid, but are you all Nicolliens?"

A laugh went around the table. "That's what outsiders call us, dear," said Harriet. "We prefer to be called magi. We're carrying on the true tradition of magery, after all."

"The Ambrosites would like you to believe we've deviated from the true path," Rasmussen said, his voice putting air quotes around "true path," "but it's experimentation and innovation that have given us every weapon in this war. Without taking chances, no one would ever have become a magus, and this world would be drained to the bone, lifeless and hollow."

"How do you become a magus? Lucia said there was a ritual."

"The Damerel rites," Brittany said. "They implant—"

"Is that really suppertime conversation, dear?"

"I don't see why not. They implant a fragment of steel, or whatever material you're bound to, into your heart. Metaphysically and literally." Brittany tapped a spot on her chest left of center.

"Into your *heart*?"

Brittany smiled, a lazy, smug smile. "It's very dangerous. Used to be only one in ten survived Damerel."

"We're better about identifying suitable candidates these days, dear, don't look so worried," Harriet said. "Excuse me, I'll go get the roast."

"I—it still sounds dangerous. Are you all magi?"

"Not Judy, obviously. The custodian of Abernathy's can't be a magus," Harry said, oblivious to how the tension in the room went up several notches. "Harriet and I are glass magi. Brittany's a steel magus, and Will is a paper magus—the most skilled of his generation, and don't go being modest, Will."

Rasmussen shrugged. "Then I won't. But I also don't like to brag."

"What does a paper magus do?" I remembered what Campbell had said about illusions, but he hadn't been very forthcoming.

"We create illusions," Rasmussen said. "Sights, sounds, even textures if you're good enough. We're the ones who make familiars look socially acceptable."

The image of Quincy slapping a strip of paper on the brick wall came to mind. "Do you use actual paper?"

"That's an Asian technique. Very few Western magi have adopted it. It's slower, but can be more powerful if you're willing to make the trade-off. Some paper magi produce illusions through, for example, origami, that a non-paper magus can activate."

"You can... buy magic?"

"Usually with *sanguinis sapiens*. There's a market in Beaverton where most of the trading gets done. A sort of neutral zone where we and the Ambrosites can do business."

My fear was wearing off, replaced by a growing excitement at finally getting some answers. "And a steel magus can fight the invaders directly."

"The steel aegis prevents an invader from sucking the magic out of your body," Brittany said, tapping her chest again. "It's what the fragment is called. Aegis, I mean."

Harriet emerged from the kitchen, pushing the swinging door open with her rear end. The smell of hot roast beef came with her. "No more talking shop, Harry. Helena wants to eat without having her digestion disturbed, don't you, dear?"

"I don't mind," I said as Harry began to carve the roast, though my stomach growled at the delicious aroma. "It's interesting."

"Not as interesting as your job," Judy said sweetly. "Tell me, have you found it difficult at all to handle the *sanguinis sapiens* transactions? I always thought it would be hard to make those deposits."

"I haven't had any trouble," I shot back, not saying *because I have no idea what you're talking about.* "My biggest problem was finding the shipping boxes for the augury orders." This was a lie. The stacks and stacks of folded boxes and padded mailers were in the corner behind the basement stairs. But it made me sound competent.

"Oh, yes," Judy said. "Those orders would certainly be a huge task. But of course you know to set the extra catalogues out by the front counter."

"Of course."

"Judy," Rasmussen said, his voice a warning.

"I'm just curious. I *was* in training to be the next custodian. I think it's only natural—"

"This roast is wonderful," Harry said, passing the plate of beef slices. "I don't know how you do it every time."

"It's the balsamic vinegar and diced tomatoes that make it so rich," Harriet said.

I took a bite. Heavenly. "I don't suppose you'd be willing to give me the recipe?" I said. "My mother would love it."

"You don't cook, dear?"

"Not well. Boxed macaroni and cheese is the extent of my skill."

Harriet gave an exaggerated wince. "I'd be happy to email it to you."

"Now, a paper magus," Rasmussen said, "could make someone believe your macaroni and cheese was this roast."

"Even the taste?" I took another bite. That was incredibly hard to imagine.

"I thought we weren't going to talk shop, Will."

"No, I really am interested." I accepted a bowl of roasted new potatoes from Brittany. "What does a glass magus do?"

"Glass magi are perceptors," Harry said. "We see traces of magic, particularly where invaders have passed."

"It's more than that," Harriet said. "We see things that are hidden, buried secrets, lost treasures. It's a relatively new kind of magic, developed during World War II for use against the Allied powers."

"You mean... invented by Hitler?"

"By magi suborned by the Nazis. We fought on both sides of that conflict."

"A secret war," Rasmussen said. "Abernathy's was almost lost. Say what you like about Silas Abernathy, he was certainly willing to give his life for the cause of magery, independent of Axis or Allies."

"I've heard of him. He said people called him a wartime deserter, though."

"What do you mean, 'he said'?" Harriet put down her fork and gave me an intent stare.

"I, um, have a book he wrote—"

The table erupted in loud argument. "I knew the book existed," Harry said. "Where did you find it, young lady?"

"It can't be," Rasmussen said. "It's a myth. There must be some mistake."

"You couldn't possibly have the book," Judy sneered.

"I do have it!" I shouted over the noise. "I pulled it off the shelf when Lucia asked me to prove I was the custodian."

That calmed them down somewhat. Brittany, who'd gone on eating, said, "There are plenty of rumors about what Silas Abernathy wrote. What's in it?"

"Stuff about his travels. He calls it his second life as a stone magus. He doesn't write much about the magical world, or the store, just about fitting wards to buildings or restoring faded ones."

"Silas Abernathy was the last of the Abernathys," Rasmussen said. "He was custodian during the war and responsible for moving the store from London to Portland, back before anyone believed Hitler was a real threat. That was 1938, I think."

Another custodian. I felt my connection to Silas strengthening. "Why did he become a stone magus?"

"He was the first custodian to abdicate. He created the ritual," Harry said. "Insisted his true calling was as a magus, and of course you can't be custodian of a Neutrality and a magus too. There was quite a fight over it, they say—believe it or not, it was before my time." He winked at me. "But eventually he had his way. Made a lot of people angry, the more so because he wouldn't choose a side, Nicollien or Ambrosite. He only wanted to build wards."

"They called him a traitor," Brittany said. "I don't see why, since he still served in the Long War. He just changed sides."

"I think he was incredibly irresponsible," Harriet said. "He had no children and no siblings, no one for the custodianship to pass to. Up until his time, only Abernathys had been custodians, and Elizabeth

Abernathy had created the custodianship to pass naturally from blood relation to blood relation, like primogeniture. It took some very complex magic over the course of weeks to figure out who was supposed to take his place. I personally think the store was miffed at him."

"It's not alive, though," I said.

"As if *you'd* know," Judy said.

"That's enough," Rasmussen said sharply. Judy cast her eyes down at her plate. "No one's ever been able to tell if Abernathy's is alive or not," he added, "but many custodians have found it a convenient fiction. You'll have to see what you think."

I nodded, and began ticking things off on my fingers as Campbell had. "Glass, steel, paper, stone. I've heard there are two others."

"Bone magi are healers," Harriet said. She stood and began clearing plates. "They can repair damage to the human body. Not disease, of course, but broken bones, internal trauma, that sort of thing."

"And wood magi have similar protections to steel magi," Brittany said. "They were the first magi. People used to think certain kinds of wood were protection against evil influences—we use rowan for the aegis. They also fight with living wood when they can. Mostly they work outside cities, where there's lots of growing things." She sounded disdainful. I wondered if steel magi and wood magi were rivals.

"This is all... it's overwhelming," I said. Judy made another dismissive noise and received a glare from her father. Rasmussen certainly seemed to have given over his earlier anger at my not abdicating, but I had a feeling I shouldn't trust his apparent friendliness. Anyone who was the leader of a magical faction must be familiar with power, and anyone familiar with power wasn't likely to want to give it up, even if it was the indirect power of having his daughter in control of a magical entity like Abernathy's.

Harriet retreated into the kitchen with her stacks of plates. "So how do your familiars fight the invaders?" I asked.

"We control them through the harnesses," Brittany said. "Direct their attacks. They're immune to their kin's magic-consuming power, of course. We use them to capture invaders, turn them into new familiars if that's possible. If not, we alter our familiars' physical shapes so they can best destroy the enemy's physical form, then we—the controlling magi—disrupt the invader's non-corporeal form, dissipating it so they can't hurt anyone and they can't return to their home dimension."

"Dimension is the wrong word, but it's the best one we have," Harry said. "Oh, good, dessert."

Harriet emerged from the kitchen, balancing armfuls of small plates that she put in front of each of us. "My famous Chocopocalypse cake," she told me.

Dark chocolate cake, rich ganache between the layers, buttercream chocolate frosting, sprinkles, and a thin wafer of chocolate wedged into the top. I took a bite and thought my head might explode from the richness. "Wow," I said.

We ate in silence—it was not the sort of food that allowed for talking—and I silently went over what I'd learned. So, Silas Abernathy had been custodian, and he'd abdicated. I definitely hadn't gotten the sense from his book that he regretted it. It hadn't ruined his life. Maybe I was wrong to hang on to the position. On the other hand, I had no desire to become a magus of any kind. The idea of having a sliver of something inserted into my heart gave me a shooting pain through my chest.

But... he'd been talking to me in that book. That wasn't something I felt inclined to share with these Nicolliens. It seemed to me that if he thought it was a problem that I, unprepared and uninformed, should be Abernathy's custodian, he'd have written something about it. And if Silas, who'd taken such an extraordinary risk to follow his heart, believed I was the right one, why shouldn't I accept his judgment?

"Coffee?" Harriet was at my elbow with a vintage enamel coffee pot. I nodded and watched her pour. I was going to need something to clear my mouth of the death by chocolate I'd eaten. Delicious, but beyond rich.

"Delicious meal, as usual, Harriet," Rasmussen said, blotting his lips with his napkin.

"Yes, delicious," Brittany said. "Why do you think Briggs chose you, Helena?"

It was so abrupt she left me gaping. "I don't know."

"Or maybe we ought to ask why it wasn't Judy." Brittany took a long drink of coffee and set her cup down with a loud *tink*. "All that training wasted."

"That's a little harsh," Rasmussen said. His fingers tightened on the handle of his cup. "There's nothing that says Judy won't someday be custodian."

"Better sooner than later," Brittany said, turning her attention on me. "You should abdicate. Not that I care, personally, that's just an objective opinion."

"Thanks for that," I said, and took another drink to calm myself. "I know I'm not what everyone expected. But the store chose me—"

"*Nathaniel* chose you. It's possible he was unhinged by the knowledge that he would die soon," Judy said.

"What are you talking about?"

"There's no way Nathaniel couldn't have foreseen what was coming."

"I thought custodians couldn't use Abernathy's on their own behalf."

Judy made a dismissive noise. "I'm sure Nathaniel did his own auguries all the time. There's no harm in it so long as you don't work for one faction over the other."

"I wasn't able to perform an augury for myself, so I doubt Mr. Briggs did. But even if it were possible, if it's against the rules, that strikes me as plenty harmful." I set my cup down and aligned the handle precisely at the three o'clock position. "And Lucia said he wasn't expecting death."

"She told you about the murder investigation?" Rasmussen said, leaning forward. That set off all sorts of warning bells. I cursed myself for saying anything.

"Not much," I finally said. "Just that he didn't know the blow was coming."

"I see," Rasmussen said. I thought he relaxed slightly, which struck me as odd. Surely Rasmussen didn't have anything to do with the murder? Unless he'd thought to advance his daughter's career rather more quickly than expected?

"Let's all move back to the living room, yes?" Harry said, pushing back his chair. I followed him into the living room and took a seat next to Brittany, who lounged with her long legs stuck out in front of her. I scrunched into the corner of the love seat and tried to stay out of her personal space. It was like sitting next to a tiger—one who'd had a large meal, but wasn't averse to taking a few more bites out of its neighbor.

"I hope you're prepared for the Ambrosite augury next week," Rasmussen said.

"I didn't realize that mattered to you," I said, realizing halfway through the sentence that it sounded snarky.

Rasmussen didn't take offense. "Disruption in either faction is bad for magery," he said. "We do both have the same ultimate goal, despite having different methods for achieving it. We all want the transition of power from Serena Parker to her successor to be as smooth as possible."

"Which is why it's *so* good you know what you're doing," Judy said.

I'd been about to admit I didn't know how to do the augury, but Judy's saccharine-sweet tones pissed me off. "It is, isn't it?" I agreed, matching her sweetness for sweetness.

"You never did tell us about your family, dear," Harriet said.

It was an effective deflection. We chatted a little longer, mostly about my family and my life before Abernathy's, until Rasmussen stood and said, "It's been a lovely evening, but I think we should be going. Thanks again for dinner."

That was my cue to stand and thank my hosts as well. I saw Rasmussen head off in the direction he'd taken with his familiar earlier and quickly bade him and Judy and Brittany farewell as well. I had no desire to see the invaders, even securely bound as they seemed to be, again.

The rain had stopped, but the roads were icy enough I had to pay close attention to my driving. I made a slow turn onto the Banfield and carefully accelerated back to freeway speed. I'd been so used to thinking of William Rasmussen as my enemy that I hadn't expected to like any of the Nicolliens. But the Kellers were nice, and Brittany... well, she wasn't awful, just intimidating. And Rasmussen seemed to have given up on trying to force me to abdicate, unless he was only biding his time. It wasn't impossible that he hoped I would fail spectacularly at something and he could use that as pressure to push me out. *Judy* certainly hadn't given up. But I hadn't liked the casual way she'd assumed custodians were free to use Abernathy's for personal gain, and I liked even less her attitude that Mr. Briggs had somehow deserved what he'd gotten. If I were going to abdicate, it wouldn't be in her favor.

The car skidded, and I clutched the steering wheel until my heart settled. How did it feel to have a splinter of metal or bone or whatever embedded in your heart? How was that even possible? I wished I knew how to contact Campbell. He was annoying, and had a sense of superiority, but I felt comfortable asking him questions, if only because he'd never lied to me. *And he's incredibly hot*, part of me whispered. The thought made me blush. That was irrelevant.

I pulled into my parents' driveway, off to one side so my father could get out in the morning. There was a dark sedan parked in front of the house, some kind of Buick. The neighbors were having a party again, with their guests parked up and down the street. I locked the car and picked my way across the slick pavement. "I'm home," I called out as I opened the door.

My parents weren't alone in the living room. Two familiar men sat opposite them, perched on the edge of the couch as if prepared to leap into action at any moment. Instead, they stood, their attention fixed on me.

"Helena," my father said, "these detectives would like to speak to you."

11

"Please excuse us," Detective Acosta said, not taking his eyes off me. My parents correctly interpreted that as an invitation for them to leave and exited the room. My mother gave me a very worried look as she passed, and I smiled, I hoped reassuringly. Then I sat on the couch opposite the detectives, perching on the edge as they did, and tried to look alert and helpful.

"We have a few more questions, Miss Davies," Acosta said. Detective Green's eyes roved across the living room, only occasionally settling on me. It made me more nervous than the thought of Acosta's questions did.

"All right," I said. I clasped my hands loosely in my lap.

"Mr. Briggs' car is missing," Acosta said. "Do you know where it is?"

"In my driveway. He gave me permission to use it."

"You didn't think it might be important to a murder investigation?"

"I didn't. I'm sorry. I knew I had the only keys, and it never left the parking lot until this afternoon, so it didn't occur to me you might want to look at it. Mr. Briggs took a cab when he left on Thursday." I extended the keys to him. "You can certainly take it now, if that would help."

"It's a little late for that." Acosta took the keys anyway. "You also didn't mention you were witness to another murder."

Brian. "Should I have?"

"Probably."

"I didn't want to think about it. It was awful. And I don't see what it has to do with Mr. Briggs."

"Let us worry about that," Detective Green said. His voice was lower than Acosta's, and there was a gap in his front teeth that made the S whistle.

"Well, I'm sorry, but I'm not a police detective and I don't have any idea what you'll find important." It was snarky, but the memory of Brian's body made me tense and sad and disinclined to be cooperative.

"Just tell us what you told Detective Sutherland."

I repeated the story Campbell had created for me. Acosta said, "Is that everything?"

"Yes."

"And you're certain of your location Thursday night from five to seven."

"Very certain. I almost missed the bus because I had to lock up."

"There isn't anything else you want to tell us?"

"Like what?"

"Like why you were seen in the victim's car Friday morning, making a large cash withdrawal from the First Security bank on Powell?"

I felt my face grow numb. "There must be a mistake. I didn't take his car anywhere until this evening. And I don't bank with First Security."

"Nathaniel Briggs did. We checked. A woman matching your description withdrew five thousand dollars from his account late Friday morning."

"It wasn't me."

"Can you prove it?"

This was starting to feel like a nightmare. "I had several customers Friday morning. We keep records of who purchases books. Any of them will tell you I was in the store from nine-thirty on."

"We'll want to see those records."

"I can open the store for you tomorrow. If that's early enough."

"It's not a good idea for you to be rude to us, Miss Davies."

"I didn't mean—never mind. Sorry."

Acosta and Green stood. "I don't think I have to warn you not to leave town," Acosta said. "We'll be at the store at nine o'clock tomorrow morning."

"I'll be there. Because I'm innocent," I said. I stayed seated because my legs were shaking and I was sure I'd fall over if I tried to stand.

Acosta and Green let themselves out. The second the door shut behind them, my parents appeared. "Helena, what was that about?" Mom said.

"They think I stole Mr. Briggs' money."

"Not that. Is your boss *dead*? Why didn't you say anything?"

"I only found out about it this afternoon, and this is the first I've been home." The last word ended on a sob, and then I was crying uncontrollably. My mother put her arms around me and rocked me gently, whispering quiet reassurances. I felt so stupid, but I couldn't stop myself. Everything I'd endured in the past three days came out of me in tears.

"They can't think you had anything to do with your boss's murder," Dad said. He sat on the other side of me and put his arm around my shoulders. "If you're innocent, they'll find that out."

"Maybe," I choked. "Lots of innocent people go to jail."

"That won't happen," Mom said. "Now, let's get you to bed. Things will look better in the morning."

"Do you want me to come with you to the store tomorrow? Those two will be less likely to bully you if I'm there," Dad said.

I shook my head. "It's something I have to handle myself. But thanks. I'll be all right."

I turned down an offer of milk and cookies—that Chocopocalypse cake was sitting heavily in my stomach—and went to my room and put on my pajamas. Then I snuggled into bed and tried to sleep. But my mind wouldn't stop replaying the moment when Acosta had said someone had seen me at the bank. It was impossible. Unless... someone had been made to think they saw me. Unless someone who looked exactly like me had withdrawn Mr. Briggs' money.

Sights, sounds, even textures if you're good enough, Rasmussen had said, and Harry had called him the best paper magus of his generation. Could Rasmussen have made an illusion of me at the bank? Almost certainly. No wonder he hadn't tried to convince me again to abdicate. He had a different scheme in mind.

I rolled over and pressed my face into my pillow and howled in fury. How *dare* he implicate me in a murder just so his stupid daughter could be custodian when she almost certainly didn't deserve it! Well, I'd show those detectives the augury register, starting with Campbell, who I was sure would be willing to testify as to my whereabouts that morning. And he'd know how to reach all the others who'd bought auguries. And then I'd... I didn't know how I'd get back at Rasmussen, but I'd think of something.

I HAD Viv drive me to Abernathy's the next morning. The detectives had confiscated Mr. Briggs' car, which annoyed me. I wasn't sure what happened to the property of murder victims that was evidence in the investigation, but I could guess it didn't involve giving it to the murder victim's employee, also probably a suspect in said investigation. And it was a nice car, too.

"Don't worry about it, sweetie," Viv said. "You'll prove you couldn't have done it and they'll leave you alone. I can't believe they could even think that. Everyone knows eyewitnesses are unreliable."

"I'm not worried," I lied. I pulled out my phone and dialed Lucia's number again. "This is Helena. Again," I told her voice mail. "I really, really need to be able to reach Mr. Campbell. Or anyone who can put me in contact with the people who bought auguries Friday morning. Thanks."

"I still say no illusion could possibly be that strong. He'd have to make an illusion of you *and* that car."

"I bet he got Judy to pose as me. She'd be happy to do it."

"I can't wait to meet her. I'll scratch her eyes out."

"No violence, Viv. Though in this case I'd join in. I really don't like her."

The street was quiet even for a Sunday morning, with only a few cars parked along the curb. The detectives' Buick wasn't one of them. I let us in and snatched the ledger from the counter. "I wish this were timestamped."

"No, you don't. Imagine what a hassle that would be."

"All right, I don't, except imagine how easy it would be to prove my innocence."

My phone rang. "I don't have time to talk," Lucia said. "I've texted Campbell and he's on his way over. He has Briggs's contact book—it was on his body when we picked him up."

I shuddered. How could so many people speak so casually of death? "Why didn't you tell me the police—"

"*Later,* Davies. We're looking into who might have performed such an illusion."

"I'm sure it's William Rasmussen."

"Rasmussen has too much to lose pulling a stunt like this. Don't jump to the obvious conclusion." The phone went dead, and I stuffed it into my jeans pocket. Easy for Lucia to say, when it wasn't her freedom on the line.

"This cash register is really cool," Viv said, poking at the buttons. "I can't believe it works. I practically expect gold coins to come rolling out of the change dispenser."

"Please don't play with it. There's actual money inside." I dropped the ledger on the counter and buried my face in my hands. "I'm so nervous I'm shaking."

"Don't be nervous. You're innocent, so you don't have anything to worry about."

"You remember the story on the news last Tuesday? About the guy on Death Row who was exonerated after twelve years due to new evidence? I'm sure his innocence was a great comfort to him all that time in prison."

The door slammed open. "I—excuse me," Campbell said, catching sight of Viv. She was resplendent in a quilted peacock-blue parka, with rhinestone clips holding her flip out of her face.

"It's all right. She knows the truth," I said.

Anger suffused Campbell's face. "You *told her?* Miss Davies, do you have any idea how irresponsible that is?"

"I trust Viv with my life," I said, "and more importantly, with my secrets. She's the only person I dared tell. I haven't even told my parents. So take a deep breath before your head explodes. Do you have the book?"

Campbell's jaw was set and tight, but he reached into his jacket and pulled out a little notebook, the kind with letters all down one side for organizing contacts. Today he wore khakis and a navy crew neck sweater under a leather jacket, none of which hid his toned chest and abs. I focused on the notebook and pretended I hadn't been staring. "I guess some people still have the little black book," I quipped, and he looked at me like I was crazy. I flushed. Apparently, he'd forgotten that conversation.

"Nathaniel was always old-fashioned. He got it from his mother. But I don't think you should volunteer that book to the detectives unless you have no other choice. Are they coming soon?"

"I hope so. I want to get this over with."

"I'm Viv," Viv said, sticking out her hand for Campbell to shake. "Helena and I have been friends since second grade. Don't worry, I won't tell anyone you're magical. I am *very* good at keeping secrets."

"Malcolm Campbell," Campbell said, a little grudgingly. "I'm sorry I implied otherwise. That was rude."

"Well, I'm sure you're not used to people knowing about all this—"

The door swung open again. "Miss Davies, good morning," Detective Acosta said. He turned his attention to Campbell, and I could see him widening his stance and throwing back his shoulders, subtly trying to make himself look bigger.

"This is Mr. Campbell," I said, concealing my amusement. Acosta was as tall as Campbell, but narrower, and compared to Campbell's lazy, relaxed pose, like a cat coiled ready to attack, he looked like a skinny, strutting rooster. "He arrived at Abernathy's at 9:20 Friday morning and was here until about 10:30. He can vouch for my whereabouts during that time."

"That's a long time to spend at a bookstore," Acosta said.

"I came early to pick up a special order, and Miss Davies was kind enough to let me browse until the store opened at ten," Campbell said. "Then I met a few friends who came in to shop, and we talked for half an hour or so."

"And you can give us their names?"

"Juliet Dawes and Ken Hardy. I believe Ken bought a book."

I offered Acosta the ledger. "These three purchases all happened between 9:30 and noon. You can ask them and they'll tell you I was here. I helped all three of them find books."

Acosta wrote the names in his notebook. "You're Malcolm Campbell?"

"I am."

"Any relation to Alastair Campbell?"

"My father." The room was cold, but I could swear the temperature dropped several degrees when Campbell said those words.

"I wouldn't have thought a man in your position had the time for much reading."

"We make time for what matters. Don't you find that's true, detective?"

"I guess." Acosta closed his notebook with a snap. "We'll check your story, Miss Davies, but it doesn't look good. If you have anything to say, it's better if you tell us up front. Easier for you in the long run."

"I didn't do it, and those people will vouch for me," I said. I was proud of how my voice didn't tremble. Having Viv and Campbell there did wonders for my confidence. I didn't feel alone the way I had the night before.

"We'll be in touch," Acosta said, and he and Detective Green let themselves out. The moment they were gone, Viv slumped on the counter and exclaimed, "I was about to wet myself, I was so nervous."

"Viv!"

"Oh, all right, it wasn't that bad, but I kept wanting to yell at them for being stupid."

"A good illusion is convincing beyond just the sensory experience," Campbell said. "There's a component that makes the viewer want to believe in the illusion. It can be very compelling. Whoever witnessed you at the bank, Miss Davies, will be certain of what she saw and unlikely to recant that story."

"Are you saying I should worry?"

"I think the testimony of several witnesses will trump that one. But I'll be investigating the illusion."

"I'm sure it was Mr. Rasmussen."

"I'd like to believe that. Rasmussen has been my enemy for years and I'd love an excuse to bring him before a tribunal. But I can't afford to accuse him and risk making myself look unstable if I'm wrong."

"I understand."

"Don't worry. We have resources, and we're not going to let Abernathy's change hands twice in one week. That would be sloppy." He smiled, and it so transformed his solemn face, lighting his eyes with mirth, that I stared at him again. Then he nodded at me, said, "I'll let you know if I learn anything," and was gone before I could do more than gaze at him in slack-jawed astonishment.

Viv slugged me on the shoulder. "Ow!"

"You have been holding out on me! You didn't say you'd met someone!"

"What are you talking about?"

Viv slouched against the counter, imitating Campbell's pose. "He's so hot it's a miracle this place hasn't gone up in flames. Now I want to be a damsel in distress so he can rescue *me*. And that smile..." She fanned herself theatrically.

"He's just a guy who... all right, he fights evil monsters, and he drives a great car, and—Viv, he's really not my type!"

"Sweetie, men who look like that are *everyone's* type. You should go for it."

"There's no going for it. He's a customer. He doesn't look at me that way."

"That's because you dress like a hillbilly farmer half the time. If you'd let me design your wardrobe, he'd look at you."

"He doesn't look at me like that because I'm just part of his job. And I do not dress like a hillbilly farmer. *You* gave me this sweater."

"That's right, I did. I still say you should go for it. What car does he drive? Please say Aston-Martin, please say Aston-Martin—"

"It's a vintage silver Jag."

"Just as good." Viv pushed off the counter and stretched, revealing a lace teddy over a silk T-shirt beneath her parka. "Let's go get food, and then we're going shopping and we're going to forget about magic and murders and responsibilities, and we might get pedicures."

"It's November. Nobody cares what our toes look like."

Viv hooked her arm through mine and drew me out of the store. "Sweetie, you never know when that might turn out to be untrue."

12

The detectives didn't show up again. I spent Sunday with Viv, and Sunday evening with my family watching *My Favorite Wife.* Cary Grant is always good for relaxing me. By Monday morning I was ready to face my job again. With luck, my newness was wearing off, and the store wouldn't be so crowded with gawkers.

Lucia was there when I arrived at Abernathy's. "Inside," she said, as if I'd been planning to stand around in the cold. "We have to talk."

I ushered her to the break room and took a seat opposite her. "Why did anyone find Mr. Briggs' body? And why didn't you warn me? You had to know they'd come after me as their first suspect."

"Cool it, Davies. It was a mistake. We needed Briggs to be found dead because eventually someone would notice he'd gone missing, and then suspicion really would fall on you. But there was some confusion about who was supposed to do what, and his body was planted without the illusion that would have made it look like an accident. I didn't know about it until you called. So on behalf of the guy I fired for screwing up, I'm sorry."

"Oh." I felt briefly guilty about someone losing his job over this, but remembered none of it was my fault. "Did you figure out who did kill him?"

Lucia shook her head. "Briggs was blackmailing fifteen people, which is a lot if you want to keep that activity secret. Eleven of them have solid alibis—plenty of witnesses to put them elsewhere at noon on Thursday."

"That reminds me. Why did the detectives think he died between five and seven?"

"Part of the misdirect. The part that worked. Did you want to hear this, or interject inane questions?"

"Sorry."

"The remaining four were all in town Thursday and can't account for their whereabouts at the key time. But two of them don't fit the profile Maxwell came up with. Too short. So that leaves us with two. We're still investigating, but it's going to take time."

"What should I do?"

"Nothing." Lucia pushed back from the table and stood. "We're also looking into who created the illusion of you at the bank."

"And when you find out it's Mr. Rasmussen, what are you going to do to him?"

"Will Rasmussen is a powerful magus and a well-respected member of the community. That's not an accusation to throw around lightly."

"I'm not making it lightly. He wanted Judy to be custodian, and if I were arrested and sent to prison for theft, I couldn't exactly work here. Who's going to be custodian if I disappear?"

Lucia's lips were set and grim. "No one knows. Judy was in training, yes, but she hasn't signed the contract. Maybe she should."

"But I don't know how to create the contract! And even if I did, if she signed it, then anyone who wanted me gone could come after me!"

"I know. It's why I hesitate to suggest it. I don't think Judy will be sufficiently disinterested as custodian of Abernathy's. You're an unknown quantity, but you seem to be doing all right. And you're far better than the alternative."

"Which is?"

"Only one custodian has ever abdicated. When Silas left, it took three weeks for a new custodian to be chosen. During that time magery underwent a serious crisis. We depend on Abernathy's to direct our efforts in fighting this war, and with no custodian... at any rate, if Briggs hadn't hired you before being murdered, we'd be in serious trouble right now. Starting with being unable to perform the Ambrosite augury." She let out a deep breath. "Any other questions?"

"I, um, you don't..." Lucia already knew I was in over my head. "What can you tell me about that augury?"

Lucia arched her eyebrows. "I know it's not like an ordinary augury, but that's all I know. Damn. If you—you'd better figure that out fast. You've got until this Friday to do it."

I stayed at the table after she left, staring at my hands. It sounded like I had Lucia's support, but at the risk of being ungracious, that didn't mean much. I still had no idea how to do the big augury, I didn't know how to protect myself against Rasmussen, and I was still probably a suspect in Mr. Briggs' murder. And there was nothing I could do about any of that. All I could do was keep the store running and pray I wasn't arrested.

I spent the day talking to people and doing a handful of auguries. Word of Mr. Briggs' murder—the one the police thought they knew about—had gotten around, and to my surprise most of my visitors came to assure me of their support. Everyone had theories about who could have pulled off such an illusion, and why. It reassured me that Rasmussen was on several other people's lists of possible culprits as well, all of them Ambrosites. It seemed Campbell wasn't the only one who disliked the Nicollien leader.

Harry and Harriet dropped by around three with a Tupperware container filled with Chocopocalypse cake and the printed recipe for it and the roast. "We are so sorry you have to endure this, dear," Harriet said. "But I promise you Will wouldn't pull such a nasty trick."

"Even to get Judy in as custodian?"

"What good would that do? It's not as if she could use the oracle to give him an advantage. She'd be sworn to impartiality."

"You don't think, her being raised in a Ni—in a household with certain sympathies, she'd be biased?"

Harry and Harriet exchanged glances. "You're new," Harry said, "so you won't know what a terrible insult that is. Neutralities are essential to both sides, and neither of us would risk losing access to them by trying to game the system."

My face grew hot. "Sorry. I didn't mean to be rude."

"It's all right, dear. You weren't to know." Harriet patted my hand. "We'll see you later, and hang in there. Everything will work out for the best."

Despite their words, I was still convinced Rasmussen was behind framing me. Maybe it wasn't to put Judy in my place, but I'd made him look foolish, and he seemed the type to hate being made to look the fool. I smiled and accepted the next augury slip. *Where will I find true love?* the woman had written on it. Her smile was fragile, and her narrow hands gripped her purse as if it were her lifeline. I stepped into the timeless silence of the oracle and let myself relax. Her question seemed so simple and yet so complex. True love, riches, wisdom—all popular *aug. pers.* questions. I found her glowing book and flipped it open, and inhaled sharply. Ten thousand dollars. Simple, complex, and expensive. I had to find out what to do with all the cash I was amassing.

Viv showed up at five 'til six. "I love you, Viv, but I don't want to party tonight," I said.

"We're not going to party. I had something else in mind."

"Well, whatever it is, it better not include socializing, because I'm beat."

Viv shook her head and walked away through the stacks. I shrugged and returned to counting the till. It didn't see much use, being only for mundane transactions, but I felt responsible for its contents. A last customer waved goodbye, and I waved back. One normal day, with no murders, blackmail, detectives, or appearances by hot security consultants who looked good in black fatigues. I felt myself blushing and locked the door with some force. Viv had an overactive imagination.

Thinking of Viv reminded me that I hadn't seen her in a while. "Viv?" I moved between the bookcases, checking for anyone who might not realize it was closing time. Not that I could imagine anyone wanting to stay here overnight, what with the cold and the smell. Viv wasn't there. I checked the break room and glanced down into the basement, calling her name again. No Viv.

I heard a rustling sound behind me and followed it back into the store. "I'm sorry, we're closed," I called out. The rustling stopped. I took a few more steps, and heard it again—like someone walking over dry, dead leaves, only this time there was the whispering I'd heard my first day on the job. I strained to hear it more clearly. It was almost intelligible, words spoken just out of earshot. "Hello?"

I walked between the bookcases, stepping as quietly as possible on the linoleum, but the whispering never became louder or comprehensible. The rustling, on the other hand, faded away the deeper I got within the store. I trailed my fingers along a row of dusty spines and sniffed the air. The smell of onion wasn't as strong as it had once been, but I'd probably gotten used to it. No perfume or deodorant to suggest someone had been here.

I reached the far corner of the store and looked up at the ceiling. There was a giant cobweb in the corner, moving slightly with the draft that came from somewhere I hadn't been able to find. Dust on the spines, cobwebs on the ceiling—I needed to take half an hour of the time I didn't have and do some quick cleaning.

The whispering grew louder, then faded to nothing. Now, who would know if this was normal? Other than Judy. I shrugged and headed for the office. Maybe I was wrong, and Abernathy's *was* alive on some level. The idea was intriguing rather than alarming. Not for the first time, I wished Silas had written a book about his time as custodian, but now, instead of wishing it for the guidance it would give me, I wished to share in his experiences. What had he felt, transferring the bookstore across the ocean? Had he listened to the store's whispers, too?

The office door hung ajar, and I pushed it open further. The room was empty, and the other door, the one leading to the stairs, stood open. "Viv, are you up there?"

"Come on up," she called out, her voice distant.

I ascended the stairs, following the faint trail of Viv's footprints as they'd disturbed the dust. A dim light burned at the halfway landing, casting long shadows that would have made me nervous if I'd been the nervous type. Which I wasn't. I hurried a little faster and found Viv standing at the locked door, grinning like someone who'd just won first place in a cheese-eating contest.

"What are you doing up here?"

"Satisfying your curiosity." She took hold of the knob, turned gently, and pushed the door open.

"Viv—"

"Nobody's been up here in years. It's hardly trespassing. And it's your store now."

"Sort of," I protested, but it was weak and I didn't believe it myself.

"So let's explore," Viv said, and went through the doorway.

The floorboards of the narrow hall beyond still had traces of wax under the dust I kicked up as I entered. The walls here were painted dark cream, interrupted only by a pair of doors facing each other, with a third door a little way farther down the hall. Beyond that, the hallway opened up into a larger space. I dithered briefly over the doors, then hurried along to the end of the hall, following Viv, who hadn't hesitated.

"This is so *old*," Viv said, pointing at a very old-fashioned switch that looked like a bell stuck to the wall.

"Don't touch it, you'll electrocute yourself!"

"Please. It's not like there's any power in here." She pushed the switch. To my surprise a few of the lights came on, though one bulb flickered and then went dead with an electric sizzle. I blinked in the sudden light, dazed by my surroundings.

White-draped shapes filled the room, low and hunched as if they were hiding from someone. I lifted the sheet from the nearest one and found a sofa that looked like it had come off the set of a World War II period drama, its maroon velvet upholstery fresh and new.

More sheets hid end tables, chairs, and a radio in a cabinet the size of a small refrigerator. I went to the window and looked down on the street, where cars passed in complete ignorance of the find we'd just made.

"This is amazing. It's like a museum," Viv said. "I wonder how long it's been since someone lived here?"

"Seventy years, maybe." There was a kitchen next to the living room, complete with oven and an antique refrigerator whose electrical cord coiled loosely on the floorboards next to it. When I dared open it, it smelled cool and clean, not of rancid meat. A little wooden table with two chairs stood positioned perfectly in the center of the room, with one of the chairs pushed out slightly as if someone had stepped away for a moment. I rested my hand on the curve of that chair's back, which was shaped like an ocean wave. "I wonder if Lucia knows about this?"

"Or it's been forgotten over the years, and we're the first people to set foot in here since it was shut up." Viv had the door of the refrigerator open and was examining the tiny freezer compartment, no bigger than a couple of stacked ice cube trays. "The cupboards are all empty. Let's see what those doors are."

The single door in the hallway turned out to be a bathroom, with a claw-footed tub (no shower), a pedestal sink, and a toilet that seemed too short for the room. The water was still running, as I found when I worked the faucet a few times and flushed the toilet. "Running water, electricity—why all that when no one is using the place?"

"I don't know. Doesn't it make you want to take a bath?"

"It just makes me more curious."

I tried the next door, the one on the right; it creaked as I pushed it open, but the light came on when I pressed the switch. The room smelled of old leather and some woody musk I didn't recognize, a man's smell, and the desk taking up most of the space was a man's desk, all wood and polished brass, like something better suited to a yacht than a mysterious old apartment.

"I'm getting a picture of the guy who lived here," Viv said. "He wore his hair parted in the middle and greased, and he had a big mustache stained with the nicotine from his pipe, which he always smoked while doing *The New York Times* crossword puzzle."

"And he always wore a three-piece suit," I said, thinking of the man from the photo downstairs. "Except he's bald."

"Bald, hairy, whatever. Look, all the drawers are empty too."

"That's not." A waist-high bookcase containing a full set of *Encyclopedia Britannica* for the year 1932 stood to the left of the desk. I moved the books around, hoping for something useful, but found only dust. I folded back the sheet covering the chair and ran my fingers over the buttery soft leather, red as cinnamon and creased with use. "I'm starting to feel like an intruder."

"I'm not. I think he likes having us here. I think he's sad his beautiful home has been empty all this time."

"I think we're both talking as if he's here listening in."

"Don't you feel like he is? This place has such incredible personality."

I nodded, and stroked the leather again. "That last room has to be a bedroom."

It was an oddly feminine bedroom, in contrast to the office. The headboard and footboard were carved with roses, as was the dresser (when I looked under the sheet), and there was a vanity table that clearly belonged to a woman. I mentally added a woman to the image of the man from the photo. "A husband and wife, maybe?"

"Maybe it belonged to one of the custodians of Abernathy's."

"Or maybe to the people who lived here before Abernathy's arrived in this country. It was moved here in 1938, and suppose Silas didn't want to live above the store?" But the idea of this being Silas Abernathy's home, once upon a time, had taken hold of me with both hands. I checked the dresser drawers—empty. "Whoever they were, I hope they were happy here."

Viv sat at the vanity table, admiring herself in the shadowed mirror. "I'd like to live here. Do you suppose the refrigerator still works?"

"Who knows?" I felt suddenly irritable and didn't know why. "Let's lock up and go have dinner. Mom's making Swedish meatballs."

"Am I invited?"

"She'll make enough for an army. Of course you're invited. I don't suppose you can lock that door again?"

Viv fiddled with the lock for a few minutes before declaring success. "I don't know why you want it locked. You might want to come up here again."

"I just don't like the idea of it lying open to any intruder."

"Do you get a lot of intruders in Abernathy's?"

"I didn't say it was rational, I said I didn't like it."

"Okay, jeez, calm down. You're acting like I suggested eating puppies or something." Viv waited for me to lock the front door and pocket the keys. "When what I want to eat is Swedish meatballs."

I glanced up at the window above the front door. I'd accidentally left it open more than a sliver, though I couldn't see more than blackness through the gap. "Me too," I said, but my mind was still on the timeless peace of the lost apartment.

13

I did two auguries Tuesday morning that ended with me stuffing yet more fat envelopes of cash into the bottom drawer of the filing cabinet. I really needed to figure out where to take it. Abernathy's had to have a bank account somewhere, right? Though I hadn't found a checkbook or anything to indicate that this was true.

It also made me wonder who actually owned Abernathy's. Custodian implied guardianship, not ownership, but Lucia hadn't said anything, and now I found myself daydreaming about possibilities over the stacks of cash. Maybe it was a shadowy cabal of magi who used the money to fund their covert operations. Maybe it was a corporation traded openly on the New York stock exchange, and if that were the case, wouldn't the stockholders be surprised at its activities!

This led me to wonder, further, who was paying my salary. When Mr. Briggs hadn't given me a direct deposit form, I'd assumed I'd be paid the old-fashioned way, with a check. But I'd also assumed Mr. Briggs would be the one writing that check every two weeks, or however often I got paid. Was I now supposed to pay myself? No doubt this was another of the things in the missing instruction manual.

I heard the door slam and kicked the drawer shut. "Coming," I said, "coming!" I hurried into the store. A middle-aged woman waited at the counter, flipping through the pages of *Master Your Potential!* that I still hadn't gotten rid of. "Can I help you?"

"I'm here for an augury," she said, holding out a slip of paper. She wore black leather driving gloves and a fur-trimmed white parka, and her hair was pale blond and done in a sort of Marlene Dietrich wavy bob.

"All right, give me a minute."

"I'm in a hurry." Her voice, a deep drawl with a Southern twang to it, sounded lazy and not at all in a hurry. I resisted the urge to shoot back a witty, cutting remark, mostly because it was unprofessional and not at all because I couldn't think of anything witty to say, and read what she'd written: *How do I kill my husband?*

I dropped the slip of paper, which fluttered silently to the floor. "I —is this really your question?"

"Is there a problem?"

"Well... yes! I don't think—"

"I didn't ask you to think. I asked you for an augury."

"But—"

The woman took a few steps toward me. "The custodian of Abernathy's swears to keep customer auguries confidential. Are you saying you can't do that?"

I faced her down. "I'm saying I can't perform an augury on this subject."

"That's also against the rules. You can't refuse someone an augury."

"Then take it up with whoever makes the rules, because I won't do it."

The woman crouched to pick up the paper. "Do you know who I am?"

"No."

"Good." She turned on her heel and slammed out of the store. I ran after her quickly enough to see her get into a rather elderly Toyota Camry and pull away from the curb.

I whipped out my phone and began to call Lucia, but hung up before it rang more than twice. What, exactly, did I expect Lucia to tell me? It wasn't as if she were custodian of Abernathy's. But what was my responsibility here? If that woman wanted to kill her husband, there wasn't any way I could stop her, and I couldn't call the police and tell them someone wanted me to predict their future murder. I put my phone away and straightened up the stack of books. I really needed that instruction manual, but as far as I could tell, it wasn't in the store.

The door slammed open again, making me jump. "You leave my father alone," Judy said, coming up to within an inch of my face. I stepped back involuntarily. "I know you've been spreading rumors. Stop now or I'll make your life miserable."

"I'm not spreading rumors," I said, feeling a trifle guilty—but then I'd mostly listened to other people suggesting Rasmussen had cast that illusion, as opposed to claiming he'd done so myself, so what did I have to feel guilty about? "But don't you think it means something that everyone seems to have come to the same conclusion?"

"As if he'd waste magic on a... a *usurper* like you," Judy snapped. "Nobody believes those rumors. You're making yourself look even less worthy to be Abernathy's custodian than you already do."

"Like you care," I shot back. "You think it's not obvious that your father would do just about anything to get you into this place? You're the one who looks like a fool."

"You don't know *anything* and you're going to destroy the store."

"I'm doing just fine."

"You are not. You don't know a thing about the upcoming augury, you haven't made any deposits at the bank, you don't do a thing except fumble around and make cow eyes at Campbell whenever he shows up."

"I don't—wait." I stepped forward, forcing her back. "How do you know I haven't made any deposits? You've been spying on me!"

Judy's cheeks were already red, but I thought she looked embarrassed. She looked me straight in the eye and said, "This is *my* calling and I have a duty. You ought to remember that."

"You only have a duty because you decided you did. I signed a contract and the oracle works through me. Again, I have to wonder—why didn't Mr. Briggs bring you in instead of me?"

"Nathaniel was unhinged because he knew he was going to die."

"So you say. Maybe it's simpler than that. Maybe the oracle told him who would be next. And *it wasn't you.*"

Judy's red cheeks paled. "That's not true."

"I don't know if it is or not. I just know I want you and your father to quit harassing me. I may not know much about this world of yours, but I know there are tribunals and I think there are laws about how magi can treat the custodians of Neutralities. Now get out of this store before I have to find out what those are."

Judy shook her head angrily. "I'm warning you, leave my father alone." She slammed the door behind herself.

I slammed my fist down on the glass top of the counter, then rubbed the pain away. I was even more convinced Rasmussen was behind the illusion, because why would Judy have bothered denying it if she weren't afraid people were getting too close to the truth? And if he were behind the illusion because he wanted Judy as the custodian, why couldn't he have murdered Mr. Briggs, too? I pulled out my phone. "It's Helena," I said to Lucia's voice mail. "I was wondering how the murder investigation was going. I had an idea I wanted to ask you about. Maybe it's not about the blackmail after all."

No one else came in that morning. Lucia didn't call back. I dusted the shelves and swiped most of the giant cobweb out of the corner, ate my lunch (leftover Swedish meatballs, even better when reheated) and searched the office yet again for the instruction manual, or, failing that, a checkbook. I toyed with the idea of counting the money in the bottom drawer, decided I was happier not knowing the total, and went back into the store to sit behind the register and daydream. I did *not* make cow eyes at Campbell. Just because he was good-looking, and had that smile that made his cheek dimple... wonderful, now

I was making cow eyes and no one was there. That was probably fortunate for me.

The door banged open. I made a promise to myself to hire a carpenter to get that looked at. "Miss Davies," said a short, round man wearing a suit that made him look like a banker. He was followed by the blond Marlene Dietrich look-alike from earlier. He was expressionless. She looked like she'd found the cream pot and taken a good long drink.

"Can I help you?" I said, straightening.

"You can help Mrs. Daigle with her augury," the man said. "I realize you're new, but you should know Abernathy's never turns away anyone with the wherewithal to pay."

"I'm sorry, I don't know who you are."

"Mr. Ragsdale. I'm on the Board of Neutralities. We monitor their activities and make sure the custodians follow the rules. And accepting all augury requests is one of the rules of Abernathy's."

"But if the augury is to commit—"

The man held up one fat finger. "Auguries are confidential. You swore never to reveal your customers' requests. If you break that oath, we can have you removed. Do you understand?"

Mrs. Daigle's smile was broader now. I wanted to punch it off her face. "I understand." I held out my hand. "The augury slip?" Mrs. Daigle handed it over. The contents hadn't changed. My face burning with fury, I hopped off my stool and strode between the nearest bookcases.

I was used to the calm peacefulness of the oracle. This time, I walked into a storm. Wind whipped at me from all directions, ruffling pages and making covers thump and rattle. It so closely matched my mood I felt vindicated. *I won't do it. I'll pick the wrong book.*

I reached out to take a book at random and yanked my hand back when an arc of bluish electricity snapped at my fingers. Swearing, I sucked on my fingertips and moved on. So Abernathy's wasn't happy about this, but had no choice in the matter? Maybe I did believe the store was alive.

I moved quickly through the stacks, looking for the familiar blue light. Nothing. The wind battered me, blew hair into my face rapidly enough it felt it was slashing my skin, but I saw nothing to indicate the woman's augury. A stack of books fell off one of the bookcases, but I left it alone, unwilling to risk being shocked again. The book had to be here somewhere.

I went to the far back corner and made my way forward, covering ground as thoroughly as I could, given the random arrangement of shelves. No lights. Just the endless wind. "Where is it!" I shouted, not sure whether I wanted a reply or not. "Tell me what to do!"

The wind blasted me, howling in my ears like a demented dog. My eyes watered, and I wiped them with my sleeve. "If there's no augury, tell me! But don't waste my time anymore."

As I finished speaking, the wind gave one final scream, then vanished. My ears rang like church bells in the dead silence that followed. "There's no augury?" I asked. My words echoed back to me as if the stacks were a vast canyon—*nononoaugaugaugury*.

I combed through my untidy hair with my fingers and returned to the front door. "There's no augury," I said, handing the slip back to Mrs. Daigle. "I'm sorry." I hoped I didn't sound as triumphant as I felt. I didn't need these people thinking I was mocking them.

"Impossible. You're lying," Mrs. Daigle said. "Ragsdale, make her do her duty."

"You're certain?" Ragsdale said to me.

"Very certain. Abernathy's rejected her request."

"I see." Ragsdale nodded at me. "Thank you, Miss Davies."

"Ragsdale! I *insist* you make her—"

"Mrs. Daigle, the rules are simple. Abernathy's must accept all augury requests. But it is not bound to provide answers. Good day, Miss Davies." If he'd had a hat, he would have tipped it to me.

"I know you're lying," Mrs. Daigle said. "You *will* provide me an augury. I swear it."

"Have a nice day," I said sweetly, but as soon as they were gone, I slumped back into the stool and covered my face with my hands. So Abernathy's could turn someone down. It was such a relief to know I wouldn't have to be party to murder, however indirectly. That had been unexpected.

The whispering started again, very faintly. "Thanks," I said, then felt stupid for talking to a building. But if Abernathy's were, if not alive, at least conscious...? "I hope I'm doing all right. I feel certain you chose me for this job, and I hope it's not ungrateful for me to wish I had more help."

I got down off the stool and walked into the stacks, which were filled with a normal kind of quiet and not the timelessness of the oracle. "If I'm wrong," I said, "I hope you'd tell me. I mean, I'd hate giving Judy the satisfaction, but if she's the one you want, I'd abdicate in her favor."

It was getting to be late in the afternoon, and the light was turning golden, making the room feel warmer than it actually was. I watched dust motes float through the air on beams of sunlight and pulled a book off the shelf, idly brushing off its surface. It was old, with a pebbly brown leather cover on which the title was impressed in gold lettering. *Phantoms and Nightmares*, it read. It was too much to hope for that this was also by Silas, and it wasn't. No using the oracle for personal reasons. I slid the book back into its place and returned to the office. The whispering had stopped. I hoped someday I'd understand it.

I sat behind the melamine desk and pondered the file cabinet. Then I looked at the door to the stairs. I'd locked it, feeling an obscure need to protect the apartment even though it was unlikely anyone but me would be in here. Now I wished I hadn't asked Viv to lock the apartment door. I contemplated the door for a few more seconds, then took out my phone and did a search for local locksmiths.

The man who showed up at the door half an hour later let me watch him mark the blank for cutting the new key. "It doesn't take long, no more than ten or fifteen minutes," he said.

"It's fascinating that you can make a key without taking the lock apart."

"It's not that hard." He showed me the brass blank and tilted it to catch the light. "You probably can't see the marks, but they're there."

I waited as he used a variety of files to cut down the blank, then tried it in the door. It didn't open. "Just missed some," he said, and in a few minutes the lock ground open. "I'll cut you a couple of keys, if you're sure about not replacing the lock. Not a great idea for security, not knowing who's got the keys."

"I think those keys are long lost. But I'll call you if I change my mind."

The locksmith had a cutting machine in his van, and in less than an hour after calling him I had two shiny brass keys in my hand and was waving goodbye to him. Then I ran up the stairs and into the apartment.

It was as quiet and peaceful as I remembered. I wandered the rooms for a bit, marveling at how new the place felt. After a while, I pulled the sheet off the sofa and folded it in squares, setting it on the floor in one corner. The velvet upholstery reminded me of my grandmother's house, back before she'd gone to the assisted living home. Her couch had been gold instead of maroon, but it had that same wonderful texture, smooth in one direction, rough and resistant to the touch in the other. I leaned back and stretched my arms out along its back, closed my eyes, and pretended I could hear the street noises of seventy years ago.

In the distance, the front door slammed. I groaned and pushed myself off the sofa. That failed augury, or whatever it was called, had sapped my will to deal with more customers. Customers who came in at thirty-five minutes to closing were my second least favorite kind, right after the ones who came in *five* minutes to closing. I locked the apartment behind me and trotted down the stairs.

"Can I help you?" I called out when I was within the stacks. No one answered. I reached the front counter and found the door hanging slightly ajar. That was strange—usually it took any opportunity it could to slam shut. I closed it as quietly as I could manage. "Hello?"

A loud *crack,* like something hard hitting the linoleum, echoed in the stillness. Then another. I heard a rushing, thumping sound, the sound of several books falling atop each other in a pile. "Who's there?" I shouted, and followed the sound into the stacks. More thumping. Someone was muttering, a deeper sound than the familiar whispering. I rounded a corner to find Mrs. Daigle yanking books off a shelf and tossing them in a heap on the floor.

"Stop that!" I dove forward and grabbed her arm. She turned and slapped me hard, making my head rock back. I didn't think; I grabbed her other arm and pulled her away from the bookcase, slinging her into the one opposite. It rocked slightly, jostling a few books that teetered atop a huge unbalanced pile.

"If you won't give me an augury, I'll do it myself," Mrs. Daigle snarled, wrenching free of my grasp and raising her hand to slap me again. I threw up my arms to defend myself, and Mrs. Daigle ran, snatching books off shelves as she went. I chased her, though I had no idea what I would do if I caught her.

"Where is it? I need it!" she panted, shoving a whole shelf of books into my path. I stumbled and went to one knee, banging it hard against the floor. Mrs. Daigle took advantage of the moment to stop and pull more books off the shelves, flipping quickly through them and tossing them aside. *At least she's increasing the randomness.* I got to my feet and staggered after her. She ran. In desperation I leaped and tackled her around the knees, bringing her down.

I crawled to where I could sit on her back, pressing her face-first into the floor. "Get off me," she shouted. "You have no right—"

"You're the one with no right, Mrs. Daigle," I said, reaching for my phone. It wasn't there. I'd left it in the office when the locksmith came. Great. Now what? I couldn't sit on her indefinitely, waiting for someone to arrive who could deal with her.

"I *need* that augury," Mrs. Daigle said, and burst into tears.

It was unexpected enough I almost let her go. But she was a murderer, or wanted to be, and I couldn't let that happen. "Abernathy's turned you down, probably because it doesn't want to be party to murder. I ought to tell someone what you have in mind, except it sounds like I'm under some kind of seal of the confessional and I'd be breaking my oath. So why don't you give up on murder?"

"Because he won't stop hitting me." The sobs were coming faster now, and I could barely make out her words. "I'm so tired. He won't stop. I need him to stop."

It was enough at odds with her cocky demeanor, her absolute surety that she was in the right, that I didn't believe her. "If you're making a play for my sympathy, it's not working."

"I don't give a damn what you think. I'm done being a victim. I'll kill him with or without the oracle's help. Get off me."

I hesitated. She sounded weary now, the drawl in her voice stronger. Maybe she was telling the truth, in which case I ought to help her, not judge her. I rolled off and stood, then helped her up. "You don't have to be a victim. And the oracle can help you in other ways. Maybe you shouldn't approach it with a solution already in mind."

Mrs. Daigle brushed off the front of her parka, which had bits of gray dust clinging to it. Apparently, I needed to sweep. "I'll never be free so long as he's alive."

"You don't know that's true. But I bet Abernathy's does. You just have to come up with a different question."

"Like what?"

"I don't know. Maybe 'How can I stop being a victim?' Or 'How can I be free of my abuser?' That way you're not telling the oracle its business."

Mrs. Daigle wiped her streaming eyes, smearing mascara down the side of her face. "How can I escape my husband?" she said—

and the room shuddered, Mrs. Daigle disappeared, and the silence of the oracle welled up around me. I took an involuntary step back, into one of the bookcases. It was reassuringly solid. "Mrs. Daigle?" I said, but the silence swallowed my words. I hoped she was safe, wherever she was.

I walked past the mess Mrs. Daigle had made and around a few corners before I saw the familiar blue glow. The book was slim, with pliant leatherette covers, and the title impressed on the cover was

Love and Friendship. I flipped it open. By Jane Austen. I'd never heard of it. Scrawled on the title page in silver ink was *Stephanie Daigle, No Charge*. I closed it carefully. It had never occurred to me that the oracle might perform certain auguries for free—and yet if it was capable of charging ten thousand dollars, or more, why not? It was like the flip side of its refusal to tell Mrs. Daigle how to kill her husband.

I returned to the front of the store, yawning against the feeling that my ears needed to pop. "Mrs. Daigle?"

Seconds later, the woman emerged from the bookcases. Her hair was disordered and her mascara-streaked cheeks were pale. "You vanished," she said. "Where did you go?"

I extended the book to her. "No charge."

She looked at it. "Is this some kind of joke? I don't want love or friendship!"

"Trust me, Mrs. Daigle, Abernathy's doesn't play jokes. I doubt it's telling you that you need to stay with your abusive husband. But—I don't know much about relationships, because the only serious one I've had ended badly, but I think you deserve better than to be with someone who beats you. And maybe that augury will tell you how you can get real love. It's just a guess. You'll have to study it and find out what the augury is. In the meantime... why don't you call a shelter? Or women's services?"

Mrs. Daigle shook her head. "It's not that simple."

"And it's none of my business. I hope things work out for you. I hope the augury helps."

I smiled, I hoped encouragingly. She didn't smile back, just hugged the book to her chest and left the store. I caught the door before it could slam and eased it shut. Then I locked the door and put up the CLOSED sign, and went to turn out the lights and get my things. That had been unexpected. And sad. I couldn't stop seeing Mrs. Daigle's face, how empty and hopeless it had been before she left. I felt bad about having doubted her. Maybe if I'd been more understanding, she would have taken the augury seriously. As it was, I had a feeling Mrs. Daigle's desperation would only grow worse.

14

Lucia called me when I was on the bus to work the next morning. "Still no word on either of our suspects," she said. "What's your spanking new theory?"

"I'm on the bus."

"That's not much of a theory. Yes, yes, that was a stupid joke. You said you thought it might not be about blackmail. What else could it be?"

I glanced around. Everyone was in the little bubble people create for themselves when they have to take mass transit. "What if it's about the store?"

"What about the store?"

"What if someone wanted Judy to be the custodian?"

"And killed Briggs to get him out of the way? By 'someone,' I take it you mean Rasmussen."

"Yes."

"I told you, Will Rasmussen is too powerful for anyone to make that accusation lightly."

"I'm not making it lightly. I think he's trying to get me out of the way." Lucia was silent. "Isn't it worth checking?"

"I'll look into it. But I wouldn't be too attached to that theory. I don't see Rasmussen taking that kind of risk. Just because I feel Judy wouldn't be impartial enough doesn't mean I see her abusing the custodianship on her father's behalf." She hung up.

I put my phone away and stared out the window. Snow had fallen overnight, and the city had that fresh look to it that would be grimy and depressing by evening. I wished I weren't so helpless in this. Rasmussen had the power to do whatever he liked to me and cover it up with half a dozen illusions. I needed Lucia to take me seriously.

The snow reduced the number of customers to a mere trickle, most of them coming in to pick up one of the remaining catalogues. Nobody was inclined to stay and chat, which was fine by me; I wanted to curl up someplace warm with a book and a mug of hot chocolate, but I had to work.

Ross Dunlop came by around eleven, snow dusting his fedora or trilby or whatever the hat was. "Snowing again," he said, unnecessarily. "It really is a beautiful day."

"You're one of *those* people."

He laughed. "Granted, I'm going to lunch from here, and I expect it to be an excellent meal. Fidorini's—you ever been there?"

"I've never heard of it."

"Give it a try sometime. The veal parmigiana is divine." He handed me a slip of paper. "Not to rush you, but I hope this won't take long."

It only took five minutes to find Dunlop's augury. "An even thousand," I said.

Dunlop dipped into his coat pocket for a large vial of *sanguinis sapiens*. "I hope you don't mind my saying, but you don't look very cheerful."

I shrugged. "A lot's happened. Two murders—"

"*Two* murders?"

I quickly explained about Brian, trying to make it sound less horrible than it had been. Dunlop whistled. "No wonder you look down. That's quite a lot for anyone to experience. And—"

"What?"

"I don't want to frighten you."

"Now I'm frightened. You might as well continue."

"I was going to say, you might see more of the monsters now that you're custodian of a Neutrality."

"That's what Mr. Campbell said. That they'd be drawn to me." The shadows seemed to come a little closer for a moment.

"It's true." He began digging in his other pocket. "I might be able to do something about that." He put a handful of odds and ends on the counter and stirred them with his forefinger. "This."

He held up a stone disk about the size of a quarter. It was smooth-faced and had rounded edges. "I can make you a personal stone ward, something that will deflect an invader. You wear it around your neck, over your navel. Let me show you." He set it flat in the center of his left palm and closed his fingers around it.

Nothing happened except the whispering starting up again, shifting position until it had circled us once, then going silent. Dunlop didn't seem to notice. "There," he said, opening his hand. The stone disk now had delicate curves in an abstract pattern incised over its surface.

"It's beautiful." I looked at him for permission, then touched it. It felt warm from more than the heat of his hand. "How do I wear it?"

"You—oh, I forgot. Do you have a pen handy?"

I gave him the ballpoint I used to write in the ledger. He pressed its tip gently to the upper curve of the disk. The stone melted away like chocolate, flowing to all sides until there was a hole driven entirely through the disk. Dunlop handed me the disk, then, ruefully, the ruined pen. "Sorry about that."

"I have more. Thanks, Mr. Dunlop, I really appreciate this."

"Not a problem. Wouldn't want you to get hurt." He picked up his book and smiled as he let himself out.

I found a spool of twine in one of the basement lockers and cut off enough for a very long loop. It wasn't pretty, but then, it wouldn't be visible. I tucked the disk under my clothes, where it made a warm spot just above my belly button. I already felt more comfortable than I had that morning.

No one else came in. I swept the floor, put away the books Mrs.

Daigle had flung everywhere, gathered up *Master Your Potential!* and took the remaining copies to the Dumpster out back. It was the most bored I'd ever been. I sat behind the counter after accomplishing these wondrous tasks and thought about calling Viv. She'd probably be off work at the diner by now, and maybe she could come over and entertain me.

The door slammed open. "Sorry," Detective Acosta said. It was a perfunctory remark, something you said to be polite. He didn't sound sorry.

"Detective Acosta. Detective Green. Can I help you with something?"

Acosta let the door close carefully behind him. He'd learned. "We thought you should know your alibi checks out," he said. Green surveyed the shelves. "Strange, how certain the teller was that she saw you that day."

"I guess I have that kind of face."

"Apparently." Acosta took a few steps forward and rested his hands on the counter. "You're still working here."

"Someone has to."

"The owners don't mind?"

"Why would they mind?"

"It's a lot of responsibility for someone who was hired less than a week ago."

"Everybody has to start somewhere. It's been hard, but I think I'm getting the hang of it."

"Interesting how easily Nathaniel Briggs was replaced." His eyes regarded me narrowly.

"I don't understand."

"I mean," Acosta said, "Briggs didn't leave much of a hole. No family, few real friends, and his job moves on without a hiccup. It's as if he was the perfect target."

"I still don't understand, except it sounds like you're getting ready to accuse me of something."

Acosta shrugged. "I'm still not entirely convinced you've told us everything you know."

Fear welled up inside me. "I've answered all your questions honestly."

"Not the same thing." He turned and followed Green to the door. "I'm telling you again, Miss Davies. If there's anything you think we should know, speaking now will benefit you."

"There's nothing—" I began, but the two men were already gone. I cursed and kicked the counter, which hurt, a good clean hurt that dispelled some of the fear and anxiety filling me. Acosta suspected me, and there was nothing I could do to convince him I had nothing to do with Mr. Briggs' murder, because I *did* have something to do with it. I laid my arms on the glass countertop and rested my face on them. Someday Acosta would give up. Probably. Maybe.

The door opened. I looked up in time to see Campbell catch it before it could slam against the wall. "What did those detectives want?"

"To harass me about Mr. Briggs' murder," I said bitterly.

Campbell closed the door as quietly as he'd opened it. "Do they still believe you stole from Nathaniel?"

"No. Maybe. I don't know. They said my alibi checks out, but Detective Acosta still thinks I had something to do with the murder. Which is true, just not in the way he thinks."

Campbell shucked his overcoat and laid it over the counter. His suit today was a dark, three-piece, pinstriped outfit that reminded me of the picture in the office. He wore a discreet pearl tiepin that probably cost as much as my yearly income, not to mention the gold watch. "I'm afraid there isn't anything magic can do about that, short of assassination."

I laughed, then stopped when I saw he wasn't smiling. "You could... do that?"

"The Long War is far more important than mundane concerns. Sometimes it comes down to that."

I remembered what Lucia had said about Campbell being a stone-cold killer when he wanted. Right then, I could believe it. "I don't want anyone murdered."

"That wouldn't help in this case, anyway. It would only draw more attention to the crime. I'm afraid all we can do is wait for the investigation to go cold. I'm sorry."

"It's not your fault. But I appreciate the sentiment."

"I came to tell you what I've discovered about the illusion cast at the bank. It's not much."

"That's all right. I was bored out of my mind until the detectives showed up, and now I'm trying not to think about being terrified. This will help."

"You shouldn't be afraid. We won't let anything happen to you." He smiled, the nice, genuine smile that made his cheek dimple. "And we have extensive resources to ensure it."

His smile, and his reassurance, eased my fear somewhat. "So, what did you learn?"

"Someone definitely cast an illusion. It was complex, multilayered, which narrows down the pool of suspects. Or would, if I were certain the magus hadn't come into town Friday morning and then left again. I'm trying not to borrow trouble."

"Who do you suspect?"

"I think you already know. But I'm trying to remain impartial. The truth is Will Rasmussen would lose a lot if he were discovered trying to make trouble for the new custodian of Abernathy's. And it's a thin thread to hang his hopes on—the possibility that Judy would work on his behalf, I mean. *I* believe it of them, but I have personal reasons to think the worst of him."

I was dying to ask what they were, but that felt like prying. "If it's him—I mean, if Mr. Briggs was murdered because someone wanted control of Abernathy's, why didn't they kill me too? I mean, they walk past the office and hear me typing, they knew I was there—"

"First, there's nothing to say the murderer had to use the stairs. Some magi can pass through walls, or transport between wards, so the murderer might not have passed the office. Second, even if they did use the stairs, they might have assumed you were clerical help. No one had any reason to believe Nathaniel might hire an outsider as the next custodian. And there's always the possibility that the murderer wanted to steer suspicion away from that motive. Killing

Nathaniel alone could look personal. Killing Nathaniel *and* a bystander would draw attention to the store."

"That makes sense. I've been alone in this store often enough that..." I couldn't bring myself to say *anyone could have killed me.* I rested my chin in my hands and sighed deeply. "Thanks for looking into this."

"It's no trouble. And some of my motives are selfish. I'd love to escort Rasmussen before a tribunal." Campbell gathered up his overcoat. "I'll let you know if anything else comes up."

"Thanks."

Campbell managed to shut the door without a bang. That was either magic, or some kind of Navy SEAL training. I kicked my feet against the bottom rung of the stool. How much longer before I could close up and go home? Too long.

I spent the next couple of hours in uninterrupted examination of the basement cabinets before concluding that the instruction manual was nowhere in the building. Washing my hands in the sink, I had a thought: suppose the murderer had taken it with him? What would be the point of that? *It would disrupt the operation of the store. Even Judy couldn't possibly know all the little details of running Abernathy's.* I dried my hands on a towel and went back upstairs. It made sense, and yet it didn't. If the murderer had killed Mr. Briggs to make way for Judy to be custodian, why would he (or she) make Judy's life harder by removing the manual?

I called Lucia. It was faster than texting, even if she never did pick up. "There's supposed to be an instruction manual for Abernathy's, and it's missing," I said. "It might have something to do with the murder. I thought you should know." It might make me look incompetent, but at this point I was more concerned with the needs of the store than my reputation. I paused on the bottom step. When had Abernathy's started to mean so much to me?

The door slammed when I reached the top of the steps. "Hel?" Viv called out.

"Back here," I said, and went to meet her.

"You want to get something to eat and then a movie?" Viv was bundled up against the cold, with a knit cap pulled down well over the shaved spot on her head. The tip of her nose was bright pink to match her hair.

"I thought you'd have dates lined up for us. You haven't nagged me about finding a man in at least three days."

Viv shrugged. "Shawn was busy, and I wasn't sure you'd be ready, after Brian..." She grinned and slugged me on the shoulder, suddenly the picture of perkiness. "Besides, you already have a man."

"I do?"

"Your adorable monster-hunting man."

"Mr. Campbell is *not* my man, Viv."

Viv hooted. "You are *blushing!* I was just kidding, but it looks like I hit pay dirt!"

"Viv!"

"All right, fine, you want to live in denial, I won't stop you." She tugged on her cap. "Anyway, I'm hungry, so what do you say?"

The temperature had dropped sharply after sunset. I wrapped my scarf over my mouth and nose and breathed in the warm, moist air while Viv's van warmed up. Her heater was erratic, sometimes blowing frigid air when the heat was cranked to full, but she didn't have the money to fix it. Viv tossed an empty Diet Coke can into the rear compartment, which had never had seats installed. It rebounded against a drum case and rolled across the floor toward me. "Didn't I stuff a bunch of plastic grocery bags in here somewhere so you could clean up your garbage?"

"Probably. I might have used them to pad the drum kit." Viv started the van and pulled away from the curb. "Let's go downtown."

"Downtown's always busy."

"It's Wednesday. Nothing is busy on a Wednesday. But all right, we can go somewhere else." She turned on the radio and cranked up the volume on Meg & Dia's "Hug Me." Talking over it was impossible, but I suddenly didn't feel chatty. I'd almost forgotten it was Wednesday. In two days I'd be expected to perform an augury I didn't know anything about. What would happen if I failed? At this point I had no reason to think I wouldn't.

I pressed my forehead against the cold glass and closed my eyes, letting the gentle bouncing of the ride soothe my nerves. It was time to humble myself and talk to Judy. At worst, she wouldn't tell me, and I'd... would I abdicate for the sake of the store, even if it meant temporary disruption? I remembered the peace of the oracle, how connected I felt to it. If I really cared about Abernathy's, I'd be willing to abdicate. And I was.

"Don't look so down," Viv shouted over the music. "What do you want to see? There's a classic film fest going on at the Academy Theater, or there's a new Channing Tatum movie—"

I turned down the volume. "You can choose."

"Wow, you went from normal to depressed in like ten seconds. What's wrong?"

"Just thinking about how I should probably have abdicated last week. I don't know what I'm doing."

"You're doing fine! Don't you think all those people who keep coming into the store would have told you if they thought you sucked?"

"It's not that. There's this big augury I don't know how to do, and I don't want to screw it up. Judy would know—"

Viv made a dismissive sound. "Who cares about Judy? You're the one the store accepted. If she had any sense of decency, she'd offer to help you. And you'll figure it out. I have faith in you." She patted my knee. "Who's a good little grasshopper?"

I smiled despite myself. "You know that doesn't mean anything."

"It will if I say it often enough. That's how things get meaning, you know, they gather it up over time like a rolling rock gathering moss."

"Um, rolling stones don't gather moss. It's what they're known for."

"They do if they're covered with glue. Which this one is."

"Do I want to know who covered it with glue?"

"It was born that way. Don't judge."

We got off the freeway and made our way eastward, but traffic was so heavy Viv had to slow to a crawl. "What is going on tonight?" she exclaimed, and leaned on her horn. "Use the other pedal, jerk!"

I watched a big Catholic church slide past, its doors open and spilling golden light onto the shallow stairs fronting it. It was thronged with people. "There's something going on at that church."

"On a school night? Insane. We're never going to find parking."

"Walking is good for you."

"Not on a night like this. My piercings nearly froze my earlobes solid walking from the van to the store."

The heater blasted hot air in my face, sending goose pimples down my arms. "We could get takeout."

"I'm sick of takeout. I want to sit in a booth and make suggestive comments about the cute waiters and eat spaghetti Bolognese until you have to roll me out of Fidorini's."

"Funny you want to go there, because a customer just told me about it this morning." What had Dunlop said was good there? Well, I'd no doubt see it on the menu. Besides, I always ordered lasagna my first time at a new Italian restaurant.

Fidorini's small parking lot was full, too. "Let's try somewhere else, Viv."

"This place is supposed to be fantastic. I'm not giving up."

"It's so fantastic everyone in town is already there."

"You're so pessimistic tonight. Give it a chance."

After circling the block several times, Viv gave up on parking near the restaurant and found us a spot five blocks away, past the church. The sidewalk was crowded, mostly with families with young children, all bundled up against the cold. I huddled into my scarf and kept a tight grip on my purse. This side of Portland wasn't a hotbed of crime, but people got mugged often enough you didn't walk carelessly.

I glanced up at the sky, sharp-edged like black crystal. I couldn't see any stars thanks to the orange-yellow light of the streetlamps, but I could imagine the constellations laid out like specks of glitter. Funny how crisp the cold air smelled, even laden with automobile fumes, when Abernathy's always smelled musty no matter how cold it got. If the store stayed that cold year-round, summer would be pleasant. Assuming I was still there when summer rolled around. I pushed the thought away. There wasn't anything I could do about it tonight, and I deserved to have a good time.

I inhaled again and sniffed the scent of rotten eggs. I wrinkled my nose. "Wonder where that came from?"

"What?"

"The smell."

"I don't smell anything." Viv sniffed dramatically. "No, I smell it now. Ugh."

The smell was stronger ahead of us, where the sidewalk widened to encircle a concrete planter containing an elm tree clinging desperately to life and a handful of scruffy bushes. As I turned my head, trying to find the source of the smell, the bushes rustled, and an animal emerged. At first, I thought it was a large dog. Then I saw the horns, curved and ridged and black like a bighorn sheep, saw the spiny back and the lashing, fleshy tail, and grabbed Viv's arm to make her stop. "Do you see that?"

Viv's mouth fell open. "Is that a cougar? What is a cougar doing in the middle of the city?"

It turned its head. Four glimmering white eyes with no pupils or irises focused on us. It took a wobbling step, as if it were trying to find its balance, then another. "It's not a cougar," I said. "*Run!*"

15

The sidewalk was too crowded for a full run, but I towed Viv after me, shoving past pedestrians without caring what they shouted at me. Then the screaming started. I didn't dare look back. Dunlop's stone ward burned painfully against my stomach. I prayed that meant it was doing its job. How far would its protection extend? Viv was helpless against that thing.

"What is—" Viv said.

"It's an invader! It's after me! Keep running!"

Viv looked over her shoulder and screamed. "It's gaining on us!"

I let go of Viv's hand and managed to speed up a little, but she was right—it was faster than we were, and at some point it would reach me, and that would be it. I darted around a couple holding hands and cast about frantically for something, anything that would provide protection. Ahead, the church beckoned worshippers for whatever it was hosting that night. I tripped and caught myself before I could fall. Viv got her hands under my arm and hauled me along. "Keep running!"

I looked at the church again. A fragment of a phrase came to mind—*places of worship to ward*. Something Silas had written about churches frequently having stone wards placed on them. I couldn't remember immediately why churches, but I didn't care. I could hear the heavy breathing of the monster and imagined I could feel it lashing at my heels. "The church!" I panted. "Inside!"

I pounded up the stairs leading to the blessedly wide doors, shoving past people, and threw myself inside, going to my knees and breathing heavily. If I was wrong about this, Dunlop's stone ward would have to protect me, and if not... I closed my eyes and offered up a silent prayer.

Viv crashed to the ground beside me. "Helena, we can't stay here," she said.

"They're closing the doors." One of the doors was swinging slowly shut, but the other was blocked by bodies and still stood wide open.

Viv gripped my arm so tightly it hurt. "Look at that."

I turned around, still on my knees, and pushed my hair out of my face. The invader paced three feet from us, just outside the threshold, its powerful jutting jaw dripping green saliva. It snarled, and tossed its head, then backed away and made a run at us. Viv and I and a dozen bystanders screamed.

The thing ran into an invisible wall inches from the doorway, rebounded and flipped in midair to land on its feet. The stairs beyond were clear of people now, but I could see fleeing pedestrians on the street beyond, and a couple of people holding up their phones to take pictures or videos. Typical. A terrifying monster comes up Main Street and the human reaction is to get something to put on Instagram.

Though... "Viv, what did you say it looks like?"

"A cougar. It's all thin and its fur is matted. It looks like it's starving. What do you see?"

"You don't want to know." My heart rate had nearly returned to normal, and I pulled out my phone and called Lucia. I left a brief message, conscious of the people surrounding us, though most of them were on their own phones dialing 9-1-1 or taking pictures. The invader continued to pace in front of the doors, snarling and tossing its horns like it wanted someone to fight. I clutched my phone, my knuckles white, and followed it with my eyes. I'd seen a tiger at the zoo once, pacing its enclosure just like this, and been awed and terrified at how it clearly saw me as prey. This thing had the same look.

A white truck slowly made its way up the street and then, unexpectedly, onto the sidewalk. Written on the side in big dark letters were the words ANIMAL CONTROL. Fear gripped my heart again. No. They couldn't try to catch it, it would kill them with a touch. "Stay away!" I shouted, moving incautiously close to the door. The invader lunged at me, and I shrieked and flung myself backward.

Four white-clad figures emerged from the doors and back of the truck, then a fifth figure, dark and low to the ground. I'd just registered its chitinous segmented body and circular toothy mouth as Brittany's familiar when it made a mad skittering dash for the monster. The invader turned in time to see the familiar bearing down on it, knocking it on its side and burying its round maw in the thing's shoulder.

The monster howled, sounding like an injured cat, and shook the familiar off. They began circling each other, testing each other like a couple of boxers who'd exchanged blows and knew to be more cautious now. Brittany's familiar undulated past, oozing up and over the stair's handrail. *What does that look like to everyone else? A dog crawling over the rail?*

The monster made a dart at the familiar, who dove beneath it and heaved up, taking the invader off its feet. It threw the invader to the ground, knocking the breath out of it. The creature slowly stood up and shook its head, and the familiar leaped on it again, once again fastening its teeth where the arm met the creature's neck. The unearthly howl went up again, making me shudder.

The familiar worried the invader like a dog with a chew toy, then spat it out and backed away. The invader stood, its head lowered and its legs shaking, and that was when a long white dart came out of nowhere and buried itself in the creature's left flank. I looked around and saw one of the white-clad figures lowering a gun with a huge telescopic sight attached. She nodded at one of her friends—Brittany, I realized—and Brittany waved her team forward. She was carrying a harness like the one her familiar wore. As I watched, she walked around behind the invader and bent to slip the harness around it. It tried to run, but weakly, as if it couldn't get its legs to go the right way.

As soon as she got the harness fastened, the white eyes lost their glow and became pearly gray. It turned away from the door and walked with Brittany to the back of the Animal Control truck, stiffly, like a sleepwalker. People aimed their phones at the pair, backing well away from the thing's dripping jaws. I caught one more glimpse of it before Brittany urged it into the truck, followed by her oozing familiar. The trapped creature howled so piteously I almost felt sorry for it. Brittany flipped up a mesh gate that gleamed silver in the streetlights, then shut the door, and the howling faded to a muffled keen.

I let go my death grip on my phone—*what image would my camera record? Not the truth, or those Wardens would confiscate every one of them.* Viv took hold of my other hand. "Is it safe to leave?"

"I think so." The Wardens were climbing back into the truck, all except Brittany, who was approaching up the steps. I let go of Viv and walked forward to meet her. "Thank you," I said.

"We didn't do it for you," Brittany said. She had beads of sweat along her hairline as if she'd been exerting herself instead of just standing there watching. "Why, was it following you?"

"Yes."

"Huh." Brittany swept a hand through her spiky red hair. "Then I guess you're welcome."

"What will you do with it?"

"Harness it permanently. Make it someone's familiar. It's a good strong one." Brittany glanced over her shoulder. A slow, malicious smile spread across her face. "Good thing we got here first."

Another Animal Control truck was approaching from the other direction. It drove up onto the sidewalk and eased forward until its bumper nosed the front of Brittany's truck. I recognized the driver as the dark-skinned man who'd been with Campbell's team the night Brian was killed. The rear door opened, and Campbell hopped out, followed by Quincy. He was again dressed in black fatigues and had a long knife in one hand. He looked around, then made straight for us. "This is our territory," he said in a low voice.

"Imminent risk to a civilian population trumps territorial rights, Campbell," Brittany said. "Though I'm not surprised you've forgotten that."

Campbell closed one hand into a fist. "Release it."

"Make me."

"I won't ask again."

"I don't have to give up my prize. It was properly captured and contained without harm to anyone. Unlike your operation. How many died the last time you answered a call?" Brittany flicked a glance at me. "Oh, right. Just the one."

"Spinelli—"

"Give it a rest, Campbell." Brittany nodded at me. "You take care, Helena."

Campbell swore at her. She grinned and walked away, climbing into the cab of her Animal Control truck. It reversed off the sidewalk and drove slowly away, flashing its lights at the remaining pedestrians to make them move.

"Is it bad, that she captured it instead of killing it?" I said.

Campbell was silent for a moment, looking after the disappearing truck. Without looking at me, he said, "It's only a matter of time before one of those things escapes containment and attacks someone. If there's any justice, it will be Spinelli. She's too damned cocky."

"It looked safe," Viv offered, startling me—I hadn't realized she'd joined us.

Campbell made a derisive sound. "Nothing about the invaders is safe. You saw what happened to that young man, Miss Davies. Imagine that happening here among all these people. To a child. Better to destroy them outright."

I didn't respond. I trusted Campbell, but Brittany's familiar had subdued the attacker without anyone having to get right up close, within knifing distance. Within distance of being killed. On the other hand, Brittany and Rasmussen and the rest of the Nicolliens didn't see their familiars' true forms, and how much easier would it be to accept them if they looked like dogs? I wasn't sure either side was completely in the right.

"At least no one was hurt," Viv said.

"True," Campbell said. "You were smart to run for St. Agnes's. How did you know it was warded?"

"I didn't. Silas wrote something about churches frequently being warded, and I took a chance."

"Ask Lucia for a list of warded buildings in the city. I hope you won't need it."

"Me too."

Campbell nodded, and returned to the truck. As it drove away, Viv said, "He's even more gorgeous in fatigues."

"Viv, we were nearly killed. How can you think about how he looks?"

"Being nearly killed makes you appreciate the finer things in life." Viv held out her hand. "Look, I'm shaking. Let's go get food."

"I'm not hungry anymore."

"You need to eat. You're shaking too."

I clasped my hands together. "Just the cold," I said. "All right, let's get food."

The crowds had already gone back to their normal, unpanicked state, though I saw a few knots of people bending their heads over someone's phone, gasping and exclaiming. A couple of people pointed at me. I ducked my head and walked faster. Viv, with her longer legs, had no trouble keeping up. "Do you think they noticed it was chasing us?" she said.

"I'd rather not find out. Move faster." The stone ward had gone, not cold exactly, but no warmer than my skin. I would have to ask Dunlop if it was still good, or if it had used its magic up.

Fidorini's was warm, almost muggy, a welcome heat after the chill of outdoors. It also smelled incredible—hot marinara sauce, seasoned meats, and the faint fresh scent of green salad. It was surprisingly empty given the crowds outside, and we got a table immediately. The server (female, short, round, and fortyish, offering no opportunity for Viv to ogle) left us with our menus, and

I immediately found what Dunlop had recommended. Veal parmigiana.

"Veal is baby cows, Helena," Viv said.

"And lamb is baby sheep, but I don't see you turning up your nose at the gyros at Athenos." Even so, I decided on plain spaghetti. My stomach was still a little queasy from our encounter. "That reminds me, though." I pulled the stone ward from my shirt and displayed it to Viv, dangling it from the long twine.

"What is it?"

"A stone ward. It's supposed to protect me from invaders." The stone was now covered in a white patina, making the curves of the design stand out more starkly.

"It wasn't much use tonight, was it?"

"I think it kept the thing from approaching too closely. Or something like that. The way the ward on the church did."

"So it wouldn't have mattered if it had caught you?"

"That's not an experiment I wanted to try."

The server returned to take our orders, and set down a couple of Cokes and a big bowl of green salad. Viv heaped her little plate high. "The gorgeous Mr. Campbell seemed to think this might happen again. You can't just move from warded place to warded place for the rest of your life. Or stay in your bookstore."

"Maybe I need a stronger personal ward. Or Lucia will think of something."

"You have a lot of faith in her."

"I trust her. And Mr. Campbell."

"What about that woman, the one who captured the monster?" Viv's voice dropped to a near whisper.

"Brittany? I don't know. I only met her once before this, and she's... intimidating. Plus I'm not sure I want a defense based on using those things to defeat their own kind."

"I wish I'd seen its true form. The cougar and the dog fighting was sort of sad. I felt bad for the cat." Viv rustled in her enormous bag. "Let's see what Abernathy's has to say about that."

She pulled out a battered but familiar magazine—Abernathy's catalogue. "Where did you get that?"

"From the stack by the door. That's a dumb question."

"You know what I mean. Those are for magi!" I lowered my own voice.

"I don't see why. You said it's as simple as asking the question and pointing to a page. And you don't know that everyone who's asked for an augury is a magus. It's just that nobody else knows about the oracle. So I don't see why I can't take advantage of it." She bent back the creased cover of the catalogue and laid it flat on the table between us, pushing the salad bowl out of the way. "What should I ask?"

"How about 'What kind of trouble will I be in for abusing Abernathy's power?'"

"You're such a spoilsport. I know." She cleared her throat, then intoned, "When will I find true love?" With her eyes closed, she riffled the pages, then stuck her finger out and touched the middle of one page. "Read it. I'm scared to," she said without opening her eyes.

I rotated the catalogue so it was right side up for me. "It says *Time and Again*, by Jack Finney. I've read that. It's about time travel."

Viv groaned and blinked at me. "Perfect. The man I'm destined to love is in some other time. I wish I hadn't asked."

"Serves you right. Besides, maybe it only means you'll find true love over and over again."

"You don't think I'm fickle, do you?"

She sounded a little forlorn, and I squeezed her hand. "No, I think you have a loving heart and you see the best in a lot of different men. What about Shawn?"

She shrugged. "Shawn's nice, but he's maybe a little too intense. I want to have fun and he's serious. I think I led him on."

"Not on purpose."

"Does it matter, if it hurts him?"

"Viv, stop worrying. You're the nicest person I know, and you wouldn't do anything to hurt anyone. Except maybe Judy, who I have to call in the morning and beg for help. So you're not the person in this room worst off."

Viv smiled. “I guess not.” She took the catalogue back, closed her eyes, and said, “When will *Helena* find true love?”

I gasped and snatched at the catalogue. She held it out of my reach, flipping pages rapidly and then stabbing at it with her forefinger. “Oh, Helena, it’s a book by a woman named Campbell!”

“*What?* Viv, you’re joking!”

“Yes, I am. The title is *Ask Me No Questions*. I guess you were right that you’re not allowed even the smallest auguries on your own behalf. You’ll just have to let your love life unfurl as God intended and wait for your gorgeous monster hunter to realize he needs you desperately.”

I threw a roll at her head.

16

"Lucia," I said, "it's Helena. I need to speak to Judy Rasmussen, but I don't have her number. Please call me back." I hung up and stuffed the phone in my pocket, where it stuck out by about half an inch. What was it about women's pants that they never had pockets deep enough for a phone? My brother Jake never had this problem. Malcolm Campbell never had this problem. Of course, he had a suit coat and who knew how deep those interior pockets were.

The door banged open. "We're so glad to see you're safe," Harriet Keller said. "When we heard about the attack... it's so fortunate Brittany was in the area."

"Brittany's the best hunter in the last fifty years," Harry said. "She's captured twenty-eight invaders, and she's only been working for seven years. She's sure to surpass the record, the way she's going."

I didn't want to ask what they thought of Campbell. "Does she ever have to kill them?"

"We say 'destroy,'" said Harriet. "They don't have life the way we do. And yes, she's had to destroy many. Familiars are sometimes hard to control—well, that's not true, keeping them under control is simple. I suppose I mean it's sometimes difficult to direct their actions when they go into battle against their own kind."

"I've never seen you with your familiar in the store."

"Familiars aren't allowed in Abernathy's, dear. Part of the Accords. The Ambrosites were absolutely determined to prevent them getting anywhere near the source of magic."

"Is that why Abernathy's is warded? Because it's full of magic?"

"Just like all the nodes," Harry said. "All the Neutralities are nodes, but not all nodes are Neutralities," he added, when I looked confused. "Many nodes are under Ambrosite or Nicollien control. And all known nodes are warded. Keeps the invaders from growing powerful, feeding off unprotected magic sources."

"I see." My phone buzzed with an incoming text. It was from Lucia, and all it contained was a phone number. "What do people do with the protected nodes?"

"Magi top off their personal magic reserves." Harry made a complicated gesture with both hands. "The Ambrosites use theirs to fuel their weapons. They don't use familiars, so they're at a disadvantage when fighting, and their engineers have developed any number of hybrid weapons, you know, technology and magic combined. I have to say I admire their persistence, even though they're wrongheaded."

"Mr. Campbell said it was only a matter of time before a familiar broke free and killed someone."

Harry and Harriet exchanged amused glances. "Malcolm means well, but he's unnecessarily concerned," Harriet said. "If it hasn't happened in seventy-three years, it's unlikely to happen now."

"Still, he's a damn fine fighter, and committed to winning this war." Harry shook his head. "Wish he'd reconsider his allegiances. He and Brittany together would be a devastating team."

"I think Malcolm would rather chew glass than work with Brittany," Harriet said with a chuckle. "There's a definite conflict of personalities there."

"Anyway, we should be going. Just wanted to stop by and say hello." Harry adjusted his scarf. "Stay safe, Helena."

When they were gone, I stared at my phone's display, trying to gather my confidence. This was potentially the most humiliating thing I'd ever had to do. Judy was probably going to laugh in my face, or at least into her phone, and I would be no closer to knowing how to perform the augury. But I had to take the chance. I tapped the number in Lucia's message and listened to the ring. It went on ringing for a while. I switched hands, wiped my damp palm on my pants, and took a seat on the rickety stool.

The ringing stopped. "Hello?"

"Um... Judy?"

"Who is this?"

"It's Helena Davies."

Silence. "Have you come to your senses?"

Oh, this is not going to go well. "I'm not abdicating, if that's what you mean."

"Then what do you want?"

"I want your help." I drew a deep breath. "I don't know how to do the augury tomorrow and I hoped you would tell me how it works."

More silence. Then Judy's laugh pealed out shrilly into my ear, sharpened by the phone's receiver. "That's rich," she said. "You admit you don't know what you're doing and yet you still have the nerve to say you won't abdicate? You're more selfish than I thought."

I closed my eyes and tried to remain calm. "The instruction manual is missing," I said. As long as I was humiliating myself, I might as well go for broke. "There are a lot of things I don't know how to do, but Abernathy's accepted me and I *am* the custodian. If you care about the oracle as much as you claim to, you'd help me instead of ridiculing me."

"What do you mean, the instruction manual is missing?" Judy didn't sound amused now.

"I mean I've looked everywhere and it's not in the store. And Mr. Briggs didn't have it on him when he... it's just gone."

"So someone stole it?"

"I don't know. I guess the murderer might have taken it, or it might have been lost a long time ago, and no one knew because Mr. Briggs was so experienced."

"No. It's a reference manual. There were things in it—look, I've never seen it, just learned about it, but I know it has the keys to creating the catalogue, among other things. Why didn't you say something earlier?"

"Because I'm having enough trouble proving I'm competent without admitting to how much I don't know!"

Judy fell silent again. I was about to say her name to make sure she was still there when she said, "I don't know how the Ambrosite augury works. It happens so infrequently I wasn't instructed in it. Whatever it is, it's in the manual."

The lights seemed to dim briefly. I hopped off the stool and paced, back and forth from the door to the first bookcases. "The manual I don't have."

"Maybe Nathaniel took it home."

"Or maybe it was stolen by the murderer."

"Why would the murderer care about the manual? If they were trying to stop their blackmailer?"

"You know about that?"

"Please. Everyone knows about it now. Nathaniel was blackmailing someone, the person either got tired of it or couldn't pay, and they killed him."

"Unless it was about control of the store. Unless someone wanted Mr. Briggs out of the way so y—so someone else could control the oracle."

Judy sucked in an outraged breath. "You mean so *I* could control the oracle. How *dare* you make such an accusation? My father is not a murderer!"

"I never said that." *In public.*

"Well, you can forget about it. And I wouldn't use the oracle on his behalf, anyway. You think I studied for twelve years to run Abernathy's just to throw that away to give my father more power? Power he doesn't need?"

"You studied for twelve years?"

"Yes." Judy sounded like she wished she could crawl through the phone and strangle me. "Twelve years, all wasted because that idiot Nathaniel thought he knew better than the Board of Neutralities how things should run. And then you come in and screw up over and over again—"

"I'm sorry!" I shouted. "I just—I came in and I'd never felt this connected to anything before, and then Silas spoke to me, and—"

"Silas spoke to you? Silas Abernathy? *Dead* Silas Abernathy?"

"He wrote his book to me. He saw I was the one who'd pick it up. I thought it meant… that I had a right to this store. But you're right, I've been selfish." I took another deep breath. "Is it too late to abdicate? For the augury, I mean?"

"If you let me sign the contract—"

"I don't know how to create the contract. That's probably in the manual, too."

Judy was again silent for a moment. "I don't know."

"Well, you're the one who's been so hot for me to give up the power! If you don't know, who does?"

I heard her sigh. "The truth is, nobody knows how long it might take for the oracle to choose a successor. I *think* it would be shorter than when Silas Abernathy abdicated, because at least I've been trained, but we can't count on that. It could be a week, maybe even two, where the store is in flux and no auguries can be sold. Anyway, you abdicating won't help with the augury tomorrow, and even if it did, *I* don't know how to do it either."

I slumped against the counter. "What happens if the Ambrosite augury isn't performed? There's no leader?"

"They have to choose a leader the old-fashioned way. Ambrosites love ritual and hierarchy. They won't leave the leadership position open for however long it takes the oracle to choose a successor. So the Ambrosite Archmagus will choose a successor from a pool of likely candidates, using criteria like, I don't know, loyalty to the cause and how willing they are to kiss her butt."

"That's pretty harsh."

"I don't like Ambrosites. They think rules are more important than people. Anyway, the point is, you don't have to worry about the Ambrosites suffering if you don't perform the augury. They'll have a leader no matter what. Are you serious about abdicating?"

"Wait. Just wait." What if that was the point? "Judy, who would be in line for the leadership if I can't perform the augury?"

"I don't know. I'm not an Ambrosite. Why do you care?"

"I don't. Maybe. What if that was the point?"

"What?"

"What if Mr. Briggs was killed specifically so the augury couldn't be performed? What if the murderer knew how to manipulate the succession so they'd be the one chosen by the Archmagus, and they weren't totally sure the augury would choose them?"

"That doesn't make any sense. Whoever succeeded Nathaniel would know how to perform the augury."

"Except *you* said the instructions were in the manual. So one of two things could have happened. Either the murderer believed you would be the next custodian, and stole the instruction manual so you couldn't perform the augury, or they believed *I* would be the custodian and counted on me being incompetent enough not to be able to do it."

"You're making a lot of guesses."

"But I know how to verify them. I have to go."

"Are you abdicating or not?"

I held the phone away from my head and looked at the display, imagining Judy's eager, frustrated face. What was my duty, here? Should I really hold onto the oracle when I knew so little, just to make myself happy?

"Yes," I said. "After the store closes today. If neither of us can do the Ambrosite augury, it doesn't matter if Abernathy's is functional or not. But either way, I want what's best for the store, and I think that's you."

I hung up before I could hear her reply, and immediately dialed Lucia. "I think I know who the murderer is," I said, "or at least a handful of people it might be. Who's in line for the Ambrosite leadership? Call me."

I shoved my phone into my pocket, once again annoyed by how it didn't fit, and leaned against the counter. I didn't want to abdicate. I wanted this store more than anything. But I had to admit that most of my reasons for that were selfish ones, and if I really cared about Abernathy's, I'd want what was best for it. And I was pretty sure that wasn't me.

The door eased open, letting in Campbell and a gust of freezing air. "Good afternoon," he said. "I've come to use my safe deposit box."

"You're the first one," I said, "at least the first once since I started here."

"It's really only a sideline for Abernathy's," Campbell said as he followed me to the basement, brushing rain off the shoulders of his overcoat. "The wards on the building are strong enough to keep casual thieves out, and the magic on the keys dissuades everyone else. But First Security Bank is where most of us go."

"That's where Mr. Briggs banked."

"It's owned by a number of magi. It provides special services to the magical community."

I turned on the light and got out the register. "What number?"

"D118. But you should check that against the book. I might be lying."

I matched him smile for smile. "I'm not completely gullible."

"Not gullible at all, I'd imagine."

"I don't know why you'd say that. I know nothing about magic and I believe everything people tell me about it."

"Being able to see through illusions goes a long way toward preventing you from falling for lies. Not that I think many of us would lie to you."

"Only the murderer."

Campbell paused in the act of extending his key to unlock the box, which was the size of a four-slot toaster. "You know who it is?"

There was a tension to his body that hadn't been there before. *I'm sure a lot of people would like the Ambrosite leader to be Campbell*, I remembered Lucia saying. *Stone-cold killer*. He'd shot Brian in the chest with no hesitation. And he'd as good as threatened to kill Detective Acosta.

"No, of course not," I heard myself say. "But it had to be one of the magical community, right? And most of them have been in here over the past week. It's possible I talked to him or her." I swiftly turned my key in the lock and pulled the box out of its slot. "I'll be upstairs if you need anything, but now I'll give you some privacy," I said, and walked up the stairs at a normal pace. Once I was far enough away that I couldn't hear him moving around, I ran.

I pulled out my phone as I wove through the stacks, listening to the distant whispers and wishing I understood them. But I put it away before I called Lucia. I didn't dare leave this as a message for her—suppose Campbell followed me, and overheard? I'd have to pretend everything was normal until he left, then I would lock up the store and wait for Lucia, and to hell with not closing mid-day.

The door slammed open, and I emerged from the bookcase warren to find Ross Dunlop removing his gloves and fedora (or trilby). Rain was falling heavily, and through the windows I saw that the cars parked along the street already had half an inch of frozen slush layering them.

"Cold day," I said. It was inane, but I was shaking at how close I'd come to revealing what I knew to a potential murderer.

"Very," Dunlop said. "How are you? I heard you were attacked."

"Yes, and thanks for the ward. I think it helped."

"Then it worked as intended. May I see it?"

I held it out to him. He fingered the white patina and said, "It definitely activated. You're lucky. Here, I'll renew the ward and you can have it back."

"Thanks." I tucked the stone disk back under my shirt. "What can I help you with?"

"An augury." He handed over the slip of paper.

"Sure thing. If the weather keeps up like this, you might be my last."

"The day's barely half over yet. I wouldn't worry."

I unfolded the paper. *How can I achieve my current goal?* "I meant my last as custodian. I've decided to abdicate."

His eyes widened. "That's a surprise. What made you change your mind?"

"I realized I'm not the most qualified person. I think it's important Abernathy's be run by someone who's trained to it."

"You mean Judy Rasmussen. But she's a Nicollien in sympathy, if not in name."

"I don't think she'll be biased."

Dunlop shrugged. "You're the one making the decision. I hope you won't regret it."

My phone buzzed. I pulled it out. It was Lucia, with a list of names:

SARAH SHORT

BILL WHATLEY

ROSS DUNLOP

RYAN PARISH

No Campbell. So much for that theory. I glanced at Dunlop. "I didn't know you were an Ambrosite."

"It's not like we wear signs." He smiled pleasantly.

"I guess not." I moved off into the stacks—

and once again found myself in a windstorm. Books flew off shelves and hit the floor, some of them cracking open and releasing pages into the wind. They fluttered around me like maddened sparrows, striking my cheeks and forcing me to hunker down with my arms over my head. "No augury?" I shouted. "I understand!"

But the storm didn't abate. Books began flying at me, battering me. I stumbled away from them and ran down the passages formed by the bookcases, ducking and weaving to keep ahead of the books. I turned around once, and a fat volume struck me so hard on the forehead my vision blurred. Swearing, I spun around and began searching for an exit. The whispering was so loud I could only call it that because it had that same hissing quality I was familiar with. It sounded like the roar of a jet engine overlaying that quiet, sibilant hum.

Then the noise, and the wind, were gone, and I stood at the center of a set of four bookcases, all facing each other. Facing me. I turned slowly, waiting to be attacked again. Instead, books drifted from all four cases, floating along the way *Master Your Potential!* had the first day Campbell had shown me magic. They wove a pattern, trailing blue light through the air that lingered the way a Fourth of July sparkler leaves a glowing line, only instead of fading, these grew brighter, spelling out words:

GRAVE DANGER

"It's not Campbell," I said, "and nobody else is in the store..." I stopped, then pulled out my phone and thumbed back through my contacts. Ross Dunlop. He was on my short list. But he was Mr. Briggs' friend, he'd given me the stone ward...

... that had activated when the invader appeared, before the thing was close enough to touch me. Or had it activated to call the invader to me? If Dunlop was the murderer, if he'd wanted to become the Ambrosite leader, he needed me out of the way as well. And how better than to let an invader do his dirty work?

It was just a guess, not even close to evidence, but it was easy enough to prove. Campbell might not be a stone magus, but surely he knew enough to tell what the ward's purpose was? I needed not to let Dunlop know I suspected him, pretend ignorance of his possible crime. If I was wrong, how embarrassing, and if I was right, grave danger might be exactly what I'd face.

"Thanks," I said, and the books began flying faster, the light growing brighter. Once again, I read the words:

GRAVE DANGER

The whispering started again. It seemed to be coming from directly overhead. I looked up.

An enormous black oozing *thing* clung to the high ceiling, pulsing and bubbling like a tar pit. Long tendrils waved in the air, stretching out toward me. It was almost big enough to cover the ceiling, big enough that if I fell into it, or was dragged into it, I would disappear entirely. I screamed and ran, not knowing where I was going.

The tendrils came after me, curving around the bookshelves in their path. I crouched low, imagining I could feel them brushing against my hair or my neck. But I couldn't run hunched over. I stood and sprinted, using the bookcases to carom off and give myself more speed. The whispering followed, surrounding me like a cushion of sound. I shut my ears to it and moved faster.

When I finally emerged from the oracle, my chest felt like it was going to explode. I managed to avoid running into Dunlop, remembering despite my terror my suspicions of him. Not that it mattered now. He might or might not be the murderer, but with the enormous invader on my heels, this wasn't the time to worry about that.

"We have to get out," I panted. "There's an invader in Abernathy's and it's coming for us."

Dunlop made no move to flee. Instead, he stepped forward and took my arm, holding me painfully tight. "It's coming for *you*," he said. "Unfortunate, really, but you left me with no other choice."

17

I tried to pull away from Dunlop, but he kept a firm grip on my arm. "I can't afford to let tomorrow's augury go forward," he said. "I wish I'd known you were abdicating sooner, or all of this could have been avoided."

"You killed Mr. Briggs just so you could become the next Ambrosite leader?" The ceiling outside the oracle was empty. I couldn't bear the thought of what the invader was doing to it on the inside.

"Nathaniel wasn't willing to fake the augury on my behalf. Thirty years of friendship, and he threw it all away for something so trivial. It's not as if anyone would know."

"*He* would have."

Dunlop shrugged and, to my surprise, released me. I took a few steps toward the bookcases—but where could I possibly go? He stood between me and the door. "It will kill you too," I said.

"I'll be long gone. It will be so tragic, too. The lovely young custodian, cut down by invaders who took advantage of the weakened wards to feed on Abernathy's." Dunlop drew a gun from somewhere beneath his coat. "Now, get back in there like a good girl so it can kill you."

I stood still. "If you shoot me, they'll know it wasn't an invader. I've already alerted Lucia to suspect you. You won't get away with it."

"Circumstantial evidence. And by the time it all comes to the surface, I'll be the Ambrosite leader and in a position to bury it again. Lucia Pontarelli may have power over the Neutralities, but she has no authority over the magi." He gestured with the gun. "Get."

I backed away, hoping I was right about the location of the shelves. "The oracle's not active. That thing can't get me."

"It will break through the last of the wards soon enough, and then Abernathy's won't exist anymore. No protection for you."

I took a few more steps. "That wasn't a stone ward, was it? What you gave me?"

"There's no such thing as a personal stone ward. I figured you wouldn't know enough to realize that. But when my expensive illusion failed to get you arrested, I had to try something more to get you out of the way."

"You paid for an illusion. It wasn't Mr. Rasmussen at all."

"A picture of you, a strand of your hair, and an origami crane bought at an exorbitant price, and suddenly Helena Davies withdraws money from Nathaniel's account. It sounds simpler than it was. But I couldn't afford to let that augury go forward."

I laughed. It sounded forced, but it felt like defiance. "Mr. Dunlop, I never knew how to perform the Ambrosite augury. You went to all that trouble for nothing, when all you had to do was wait for me to fail tomorrow. But why did you weaken Abernathy's wards?"

"Are you hoping to stall? I'm not sure why."

A shot echoed through the still air, then another. Dunlop dropped his gun and clutched his shoulder. Then he collapsed.

"She was waiting for that," Campbell said.

I sagged against the nearest bookcase, holding tight to its shelves so I wouldn't fall. "I forgot you were here."

"Really? Then what were you stalling for?" Campbell stuck Dunlop's gun in his waistband at the small of his back and crouched over the bleeding man. "He'll live to stand trial, if you were wondering."

"Is it bloodthirsty of me that I don't care? And I was just hoping to be able to hide in the stacks." I looked up at the ceiling, where a heat haze was, against all reason, bleeding across its high surface. I pointed. "What's that? Please tell me—"

"There's an invader there. A big one. Incorporeal, and if Dunlop weakened Abernathy's wards—why did he do that? I missed the first part of your conversation."

"He murdered Mr. Briggs so he could be the Ambrosite leader."

Campbell stood, taking off his suit coat and tossing it over the counter. "If the wards were weakened, he could have traveled between them and somewhere else. Into the basement and out again, without knowing you were in the store." He stuck his own gun into his waistband and stood, hands on hips, staring up at the invisible monster. "I think we may be doomed."

"Can't you fight it?"

"Something that size requires several steel magi working together. I can call for a team, but it will be too late for Abernathy's. It will consume the store's magic, and it will kill the oracle. You need to get out of here."

"No."

Campbell looked over at me. "What?"

"This store is my responsibility, and I'm not leaving until it's out of danger."

"I could toss you out the door and lock it."

"I have the only keys."

Campbell swore. "Well, if you're not leaving, I hope you have some idea of how to fight it."

The whispering rose again, and by the look on his face, Campbell could hear it too. "What is that?"

"I think it's Abernathy's, trying to communicate." I ran to the counter and tore a sheet from the back of the ledger. "Quick, write an augury!"

Campbell took the paper and scrawled a few lines on it. "Why?"

"So we can get inside." I folded the paper without looking at it and took Campbell's hand. It was firm and warm and much bigger than mine, and I locked my fingers with his and said, "Don't let go." I pulled him forward with me into the stacks.

It was like stepping into a bowl of Jell-O, cold and squishy and resisting my movements. I immediately felt a tug on my arm as Campbell met even more resistance than I did. I took another step, dragging Campbell with me. He weighed a ton. I ducked my head, pushing forward as if facing a stiff headwind, and said quietly, "If you want to live, let us in."

Then the pressure was gone, and I stumbled and fell to my knees, still clutching Campbell's hand. I heard him land hard on the linoleum and curse. I looked up. The enormous black monster still clung to the ceiling, its tendrils flailing as if seeking something out.

Campbell pushed himself to his feet and drew a long steel knife from his left sleeve. "I wish I hadn't wasted bullets on Dunlop," he said. "Though I still wouldn't have enough steel rounds to kill it." He shifted the knife to his left hand and drew his gun with his right, then shot thirteen times into the thing's center. It howled the way the "cougar" had, and struck at us. Campbell grabbed me and bore me to the ground.

"Now what?" I said. I had to speak loudly because the whispering was back, and it was getting louder.

"Now I see how much damage I can do before it kills me." Campbell climbed one-handed to the top of one of the eight-foot-tall bookcases, kicking books out of the way and shoving a whole stack of them to the floor. The high ceiling was still low enough that he had to crouch to avoid brushing his head against the invader's pulsing body. Wielding his knife like a sword, he slashed at the tendrils, which reached to envelop his body.

I stood there like an idiot, watching Campbell fight for both our lives, wishing I knew what I could do. A tendril wrapped around Campbell's leg, and he struck it off, tossing it to the ground near me. I kicked it, not thinking until too late that that might be a stupid thing to do. It curled around my shoe and squeezed. I screamed and kicked my shoe off, sending it flying into a shelf and caroming off the books. Instantly the wind started again, and books flew in all directions. The howl of the no-longer-whispers echoed in my ears. Now they made sense. *Help*, the voices said, hundreds of voices all clamoring at me until I covered my ears and cried out.

Distantly, past the sound of the howl, I heard Campbell shout my name, and hoped I wasn't fatally distracting him. "What do I do?" I cried. "Tell me how to help you!"

"*... oracle... hands...*"

"I know I'm your hands! I don't know how to stop that thing!"

"*... oracle... hands... body...*"

I felt so small and stupid. Here was this great, incomprehensible thing, and it was trying to talk to me and I had no idea what it meant. "You want me to be your body?"

Liquid trickled from my ears and my nose. The howl was tangible, pressing in on me from all sides, filling me until I felt swollen, like a water balloon filled past its capacity. I screamed, and exploded.

I was empty, light—no, filled with light that exerted the faintest pressure on my immaterial body. I opened my eyes. Bookcases drifted past beneath me, or at least past the part of me that was consciousness, because I couldn't see my body at all. I looked up. The vast swollen thing that was the invader's body still clung to the ceiling, but it was overlaid with a field of black, studded with silver stars. It should have been beautiful, but it felt so wrong I shied away from it, unwilling to touch it.

The invader noticed me. Its attention shifted from the small figure it had nearly engulfed to focus on me. Black oozing tendrils reached out. I couldn't let them touch me. So I reached past them for the field of stars, wove my fingers through it, and *pulled*.

It felt like peeling an octopus off a rock probably would, all these points of contact with the ceiling resisting my pull like thousands of tiny suction cups. I wiggled my fingers even more closely and found the thing shriveled wherever I touched it. Then the first of the black tendrils reached me, and I felt a cold so intense it burned. I screamed, but pulled harder, because I knew if I gave up, it would kill me.

A line of silver light slashed through the tendril wrapped around me. I couldn't see Campbell as more than a small shadow, much smaller than me, but his knife wove a silver pattern around the body of the invader. Wherever it touched, the body fell to pieces. I tugged harder and left him to his work. I could see its face now—not a real face, but a shape that looked back at me, that was the focus of its consciousness. It looked furious, and terrified.

I snarled at it, baring my teeth like an animal protecting its young. The oracle was mine, or I was its, and I couldn't tell the difference between us anymore. Maybe there was no difference. I braced my immaterial, invisible body against half a dozen bookcases, pulled hard, and heard a tearing sound as the thing came slowly, grudgingly free from the ceiling. I shouted joyfully and began gathering it in, piling it up like a tablecloth being bundled away haphazardly for storage. The black tendrils flailed frantically, unable to decide who to go after. More of them fell, severed by the silver knife.

As I bundled the field of stars to myself, it shrank, vanishing in my hands. Distantly I heard a scream of terrible rage and sorrow. Then it was gone. The black tendrils shriveled and collapsed on themselves, falling to the floor and disappearing as they went, and the invader's body went limp and pale, then vanished. I hung wavering in the air above the oracle—or was I the oracle? It was all very confusing. And I wasn't sure what to do next.

I drifted across the shelves, greeting the books, who were mostly grumbling about being disturbed. I patted a few of them in reassurance, then did a back roll, enjoying the way this body moved so fluidly. I still couldn't see myself, but I discovered that didn't bother me. All that mattered was the freedom, and the peace of finally being myself.

I saw Campbell clearly now, a small figure crouched on the floor over someone lying prone there. Idly I wondered who it was, and reached out to prod the woman so she'd roll over. My immaterial hand went through her without disturbing her. That's right; I needed hands to do my work. She was probably the hands.

No, that was wrong. *I* was the hands. So why was I up here?

Panic struck, and I fluttered away in a wind of my own making. Helena. I was Helena, and that was my body. I didn't know how I'd gotten free of it and I certainly didn't know how to get back into it. I tried to take a calming breath and freaked out a little more when I discovered I didn't have lungs. Finally I relaxed and drifted back toward my body.

Campbell was leaning over my body, which was now on its back —oh, good, he was giving me CPR, of course he knew how to do that. Maybe that would draw me back. I waited. Nothing happened. I started to panic again. It wasn't working and I was going to be trapped within the oracle forever. Maybe that's how the oracle had started, one person leaving her body and never returning, then another and another—

Stop it. You can do this. No giving up. What would Viv think if she knew you were behaving this way? I drifted lower until I was pressed right up against my body, between it and Campbell. What had happened? There had been pressure, and my nose bled—there were still traces of blood on my cheek—and then I'd exploded. So maybe I needed to reverse that.

I drew myself in as small as I could get, then smaller, picturing myself shrinking the way the invader had. If I could be small enough, I could fit back into my body, probably—

I blinked. Then I drew in a breath and started coughing uncontrollably. Hands supported me to a sitting position. "Thank God," Campbell said. "I thought you were dead."

"I might have been if I hadn't figured out how to come back."

"Come back? From where?"

"From being the oracle, I think. I'm guessing no one's done that before."

"Not to my knowledge. I had no idea Abernathy's had that kind of power. That creature of light was you? You destroyed that invader single-handedly."

"Not really. I had your help."

"I'm not sure I did much, but you're welcome."

I realized he still had his arms around me, and disentangled myself as gracefully as possible, which wasn't very. I needed his assistance to stand and walk the few steps out to the front counter.

Books lay in drifts all around us. "That's going to be quite the mess to clean up," Campbell said.

"Not really. Abernathy's likes it that way."

"Well, I'd be happy to help, if you want. If you tell me what happened to Dunlop—oh, damn." There was a dark smear of blood on the linoleum, but Dunlop was nowhere in sight. "I knew I should have shot to kill, but I thought he might need to go to trial."

"I'm glad you didn't kill him. I don't need to see three murders in one week."

Campbell smiled at me. His dimple really was devastating. "You've just turned into the embodiment of the oracle. I doubt anything as mundane as death could faze you."

I leaned on him a little more than I probably needed to. "I'd rather not find out."

18

"I think I've reconstructed it all," Lucia said, lounging against the office desk. "Dunlop wanted to be the next head of the Ambrosites here, and went to Briggs to convince him to give a fake augury. Briggs declined. Dunlop weakened the wards so he could travel between them and returned to kill Briggs, figuring the weakened wards would allow the invaders to destroy the oracle. Don't know whether he knew you were in line to be the next custodian or not, but he certainly seems to have believed Briggs' death would upset things enough to prevent the augury."

"And then, when it turned out there was still a custodian and the invaders weren't acting fast enough, he tried to get me arrested and then killed." I played with the string of paper clips Viv had made. "You know he came in here offering to 'strengthen' the wards? When what he was probably doing was weakening them further."

"You know so much, why don't you tell me the rest of the story?"

"Sorry. I'll shut up."

"*Anyway*, by the time he learned you were abdicating, it was too late to fix the wards, so he had no choice but to go forward with letting the invaders suck the magic out of Abernathy's. I think he suspected you were on to him, because of the fiasco with his so-called personal ward, but that was only guilt talking. He couldn't have guessed you wouldn't have the sense to mention it to someone."

"Hey, I'm still new to all of this. And Mr. Dunlop was incredibly lucky no one caught on, because he had so many plans going all at once. Like stealing the instruction manual."

"We're having his home searched. If he has it, we'll find it."

"That's good, but I can wait."

Lucia arched an eyebrow. "You can? I thought this was urgent."

"Not the way it used to be."

It had been unexpectedly difficult, the previous night, to tell Judy I wasn't abdicating after all. Rasmussen had been furious, Judy resigned, as if she'd expected my change of heart. But with dozens of magi running around Abernathy's, restoring the wards and cleaning up the books, my story of the enormous invader and its destruction had been very convincing.

"I know there's still a lot I have to learn," I'd said, "but I've done something no one else has ever managed—something no one believed was possible. And if that doesn't make me Abernathy's custodian by right, I don't know what would."

"You'll regret this," Rasmussen had said.

"Is that a threat, Mr. Rasmussen?"

"A prediction." And he'd swept Judy out of the store in his wake. Judy had looked like she wanted to say something, but only followed her father, head bowed. I'd followed them as far as the door, caught it before it could slam, and watched them drive away. Maybe he was right. Maybe I'd still made the wrong decision. But I felt at peace the way I hadn't all week.

"Well, I guess you know best," Lucia said, bringing me back to the present. "Any sign of those detectives?"

"None. I think they've run out of reasons to come after me. Though I wouldn't be surprised if Detective Acosta put me on some kind of watch list. Is there any chance he might, I don't know, sense something unusual about me?"

"Some people are more aware of magic and the invaders than

others. What you might call 'second sight.' But sometimes suspicion is just suspicion. Don't read too much into it."

"All right. I plan to be grateful not to be under scrutiny anymore."

Lucia pushed off the desk and headed for the door. "When are they arriving?"

"At noon exactly. I'm nervous about meeting the Archmagus. What's she like?"

"I've never met her, but I know she's a powerful wood magus who defended Hokkaido single-handedly for seven years. And she's tough enough to have risen in the Ambrosite ranks fairly quickly. I don't think she's more than fifty." Lucia shrugged. "I wouldn't worry about it. After that invader, I'm sure she'll be easier to handle than a kitten."

"Wait," I said. Lucia paused with her hand on the doorknob and gave me an inquiring look. "I still don't know why Mr. Briggs hired me. He seemed awfully nervous when I was signing the employee agreement, like he was afraid he might be in trouble."

"Because he *was* going to be in trouble. The Rasmussens, for one, would have made his life hell when they found out."

"But that doesn't explain why he did it in the first place."

Lucia shrugged again. "Because he wanted a change. Because he needed someone who wouldn't interfere with his blackmail. Because he had a premonition. Take your pick. It's not like he's in a position to tell us."

"I guess. I don't like mysteries, that's all."

"With luck, that will be the last one you have to deal with." Lucia shut the door loudly behind her.

I leaned back in my chair and closed my eyes. It was tempting to think Mr. Briggs had intended me to be the next custodian, especially since Silas seemed to have written his book for me. But if he'd known that much, didn't that suggest he'd known Dunlop planned to kill him? And I just couldn't imagine anyone willingly turning their back on the knife like that. Lucia was right; I couldn't ask him, so all I could do was guess. And ultimately it didn't matter.

My phone chimed an alarm. Fifteen minutes to twelve. I went into the store and did a little nervous, unnecessary tidying up, setting the

CLOSED sign in the window to dissuade ordinary customers. The augury was another thing I was guessing at, and if I was wrong, I was going to look like a fool *and* cause upheaval among the Ambrosites. I wandered among the bookcases, straightening the shelves and squaring off stacks of books. An old Nancy Drew book caught my eye, its binding clean and fresh. It was probably worth money all by itself and not just as an augury. Dunlop had been right about one thing: you never knew where you'd find something interesting.

The door slammed open. I walked back to the counter, not hurrying but not taking my time, either. A small crowd stood inside the door, which Campbell was closing. Two more men and a woman surrounded a group of three in the center of their protective circle. I didn't know any of them except Campbell, who smiled briefly at me before turning impassive.

One of the women in the center had shining blond hair pinned high on her head and wore an elegant pantsuit with pearls. I guessed she was Serena Parker, local leader of the Ambrosites for a few minutes longer. The Asian man standing next to her, holding a slim laptop, wore a suit as expensive as Campbell's. He was speaking to the woman, also Asian, who was dressed in red robes—not a kimono, but the sort of costume a monk in a medieval movie might wear. Though I didn't think any monk would dress in such garish colors. Her black hair was threaded with silver, and there were tiny lines beside her eyes. She turned her attention on me, and bowed. "Yamane Mitsuko," she said in a sweet, lilting voice.

I did my best to mimic her bow. "Helena Davies, my lady Archmagus, and welcome to Abernathy's."

"Thank you for your welcome," Yamane said. She had no trace of an accent, but I'd expected that. Campbell, in preparing me on the etiquette for this visit, had said wood magi were usually fluent in several languages. "You are prepared?"

I smoothed my skirt over my thighs. "I am."

Yamane held out a hand toward the man, who reached inside his suit coat and removed a small envelope, the kind you get with elaborate floral arrangements. He put it into her hand, and she extended it to me. I took it with both hands and bowed again. "Excuse me." Without opening the envelope, I turned and entered the oracle.

The stillness was that of tens of thousands of books holding their breath, waiting. I walked until I reached the center of the oracle, the place where four bookcases faced each other. I couldn't help glancing up at the ceiling, but it was bare and high and free from monsters. I set the unopened envelope on one of the shelves, stepped back, and closed my eyes.

"I don't know all your rules yet," I said. "I know there are certain questions you won't answer. But you spoke to me, and I think you know how to answer this question if it's what you choose to do. So... show me."

I heard the shifting of covers across covers, like the movement of a vast snake sliding its dusty coils across the shelves. Gradually, lines of light played across the inside of my eyelids. Angles appeared, outlining books, then curving lines spelled out titles on the spines and covers. Still with my eyes closed, I held out both hands and felt a book settle into them. Then another. Then another. The pile grew, and yet I had no trouble holding it, as if the books were supporting their own weight.

The golden lines faded. The shifting stopped. Something nearby breathed out, a hot, dry wind that brushed my cheeks and filled the air with the scent of fresh apples. I opened my eyes. Ten books balanced neatly on my outstretched hands, but not in a perfectly aligned pile. I looked at the spines, let my eyes go unfocused briefly, and the augury sprang into view. I let out a long, relieved breath. I'd half expected that to fail.

I cradled the stack in the crook of my arm, retrieved the envelope, and walked back through the stacks. The books still weren't as heavy as they should have been, and I hoped that would stay the case until I could set them on the counter. One of them was an encyclopedia of North American birds that probably weighed ten pounds all by itself.

No one had moved in however long I'd been gone. It felt like ten minutes; it might have been an hour. I'd never worked out whether time ran at exactly the same speed within the oracle, but if it didn't, it wasn't that far off the outside world. I set the books on the counter and straightened a few so they fell into the proper alignment. "This is your augury."

The man said something in what I guessed was Japanese. He sounded cranky.

Parker said, "It will take days to go through all those books. Are you sure you've done it properly?"

"Absolutely. And you won't need to go through the books. The augury is simpler than that."

"It doesn't look—"

Yamane held up a hand for silence. She walked toward the counter. I saw, as her feet kicked her robes out of the way, that she was wearing Converse sneakers, and I quickly looked away before anyone could see me smile.

Yamane ran her finger down the spines, top to bottom, touching the first letter of each title, all of them aligned perfectly with each other. "Is the oracle Japanese, do you think?" she said.

"I don't know, ma'am. I just know this is how titles are written in English-language books, and it's convenient for spelling things out, don't you think?"

"Agreed." She beckoned to Parker and the man. "See here."

The first letter of each title, reading down, spelled out a name: R Y A N P A R I S H.

Yamane nodded once, then bowed to me. I bowed in return. "The transfer," she said to her companion, who set his laptop on the counter. It was the strangest contrast to the Victorian cash register.

The man began typing, paused, entered a few more letters and numbers, then turned the screen to face me. "Is the amount satisfactory?"

I swallowed. I'd never seen that many zeroes after a number before. "That's fine." I hoped Abernathy's didn't mind me making that decision, but I had a feeling now that money was irrelevant to the oracle.

The man hit Enter, and a little status bar sprang up, gradually filling up with blue. I watched, holding my breath as if that would keep something catastrophic from interfering with the money transfer. But nothing did. The bar disappeared, and TRANSFER COMPLETE blinked on the screen a couple of times. The man shut the laptop and returned to Yamane's side.

"Our thanks to Abernathy's for its service," she said, and turned to leave.

Two of the flankers opened the door and stepped out ahead of her, scanning the street for threats. Yamane seemed to take this for granted. She and her companions left, followed by the other flankers and Campbell, who brought up the rear. He paused in the doorway, and turned to look at me.

"I see you've found your footing," he said with a smile.

"I hope so. I still have a long way to go. But I feel more confident now."

He shook his head, still smiling. "You have unsuspected depth."

"Like C. K. Dexter Haven," I said without thinking.

"*The Philadelphia Story?*"

I gaped. "You know it? It's one of my favorites. Though I think it has questionable morals."

"You mean the suggestion that men aren't responsible for their own philandering? I agree." He glanced over his shoulder. "You really do have unsuspected depth," he added, and closed the door gently behind him.

I watched him through the window as he hurried to catch up to the Archmagus's party. Handsome, charming, and he had excellent taste in films. *I wonder if we might not become friends, after all.*

I left the CLOSED sign where it was for the moment. I felt I'd earned a break, and it was lunchtime. I heated up my lunch (shrimp scampi, not the greatest reheated) and sat down to eat, but I felt restless, and the break room was really cold. Maybe the location of the thermostat was in the missing instruction manual, in which case I wished I hadn't been so cavalier about not needing it. After a moment's reflection, I gathered up my plate and went upstairs to the apartment.

It was warmer there, and the rooms smelled of the same apples

I'd smelled in the oracle, not a whiff of onion anywhere. I sat at the little table and ate, feeling my tension bleed away into the walls. Golden light filled the air, playing across the velvet sofa and the white-sheeted figures surrounding it. I finished eating, rinsed off my plate, and lay down on the sofa, running my fingers across the curve of its back. The ceiling was higher than I was used to, high and white and not at all grimy despite how long it had lain untended. If Silas had lived here, he must have been so happy.

I rolled off the sofa and went to look out the window at the cars passing below. The parking spot in front of Abernathy's was unoccupied. No one was clamoring for my attention. Warm sunlight touched my hands where they rested on the sill. *You could put a plant here, it's so deep. Maybe a geranium.*

I turned around and leaned against the window so the sun could warm my back. Then I took my phone out and selected a number. "Lucia, it's Helena," I said. "Who owns the apartment above the store?"

"I DIDN'T KNOW how much crap you have, or I would have stayed home," Jake said. He carried a cardboard box as big around as his arms could go, and pretended it weighed as much as he did.

"Those are clothes, and you can blame Viv for how many there are. Put it in the bedroom—that's on the other side. Thanks." I passed him with my own armload, a stack of unopened boxes containing plates and bowls and glasses, and set them on the kitchen counter. Mom was already busy unloading some of our other purchases. She'd gone a little nuts shopping for me, getting all sorts of gadgets and things for my first kitchen. I didn't want to remind her I didn't know how to cook.

"Helena, come look at this," my father said from the living room. He'd installed a TV, not too big, over the radio cabinet, and set up some shelves for my DVD player and other "essentials" to the modern entertainment experience. "I didn't want to obscure the radio, even if it doesn't work. It's still a beautiful conversation piece."

"I helped," Viv said. "Well. I held tools and gave my opinion about where to put that chair."

"I love it. Isn't it weird how the TV doesn't look out of place? I was afraid it would clash." The room still looked vintage, but the TV gave it more of a retro look. My computer, which I'd set up in the study, did look out of place, but I figured *I* looked out of place in that man cave, so Silas would just have to endure. It had been his apartment, after all, and I liked to pretend he knew I'd taken it over. Lucia hadn't told me any more than that it had belonged to him, and I wasn't sure I wanted any more details. Pretending was more fun.

A crash echoed up the stairs. Jake came down the hall with another box. "They broke through," he said. "Looks like they'll fix that outer door today. How come they're working on Sunday, again?"

"I couldn't have stayed here if they didn't," I said, ignoring the rest of his comment. What my family didn't know was that the crew working on restoring the bricked-over rear entrance to Abernathy's was made up of Wardens, most of them magi. Their biggest problem was hiding the magical aspects of their construction efforts from my family. "It's going to be so much more convenient."

"I'll be more comfortable if you install an alarm system," Dad said. "I'd be happy to pay for it if your boss won't."

"They will. But thanks." The alarm system, also semi-magical, had been put together by a team of Ambrosites who'd brought with them a fat yellow envelope. Inside were the keys to Mr. Briggs' Civic and a message in an elegant cursive hand: *The police discovered the title is in the name of Erica Withers, whom they believe to be Abernathy's owner. Consider it yours for the duration. No assassination required.* I hadn't seen Campbell since the day of the Ambrosite augury, and now I wished I knew how to reach him, to thank him. But I hadn't been able to nerve myself up to asking Lucia for his number. It felt bold, and in general I left bold to Viv.

We all trooped back down for another load, but there wasn't much left—another box of clothes, a few odds and ends. My framed samurai and geisha, which I intended to hang in the study. I'd left all my stuffed animals in my old room; it felt like saying goodbye to another life, starting something new.

Dad disappeared into the study, muttering something about a wireless network. I wasn't sure I needed that, but I didn't like to disappoint him when he was so happy to do it. Jake followed him. I left Viv hanging clothes in my closet and followed Mom into the kitchen, where she was still putting things away. "It's a nice kitchen, isn't it?" I said.

"It's a *wonderful* kitchen. It's so well laid out, and this gas range... they don't make them like this anymore. I still think you should get a chest freezer. I know how you eat. You need a place to put your frozen pizzas."

"I'll think about it. I still haven't gotten my first paycheck yet." I leaned against the table and watched her arrange my new dinnerware, red earthenware I hoped was unbreakable. "I'm a little afraid of all this. I didn't actually think they'd let me use the apartment."

"You're taking on a huge responsibility. It's only fair they give you rewards as well." Mom put away a final plate and came to give me a hug, squeezing tightly. "I'm so proud of you."

"Prouder than of Cynthia?"

"You know I don't play favorites. But... things always came easily for Cynthia. She always knew what she wanted to do. I'm glad to see you with some direction, finally." She released me with a grin. "Not that you were aimless. But you know what I mean."

"I do." I picked up a wire whisk and brandished it. "What exactly do you picture me doing with this?"

"Scrambled eggs. Batter for French toast. You have to learn to cook sometime."

I pretended to hunt through the boxes. "Where's that ad for the chest freezer?"

Viv appeared in the doorway. "I'm getting rid of some of your clothes. The thrift store will be pleased with your generous donation."

I moved toward her, picking up speed as she turned and ran. "I have to okay everything, Viv! Don't you dare throw out my things!"

"All right, but you need to reduce your wardrobe by at least half. It's called frugal living and it will make you happier."

"Both of you move those clothes and let me make the bed," Mom said, but she was smiling.

Jake poked his head in the doorway. "Hel, there's someone downstairs for you. I think it's a customer."

"Can't be. We're closed on Sunday."

I went downstairs and into the store, where to my surprise I found Judy, dressed in a full-length gray wool coat and matching tam. She carried a large tote from Barnes & Noble and looked annoyed. "What do you want?" I said, feeling defensive.

"I brought you this. It was in Ross Dunlop's house." She pulled a large book out of the tote. It was plainly bound in drab green buckram, with no dust jacket, and had to be nearly two inches thick. I took it from her and flipped it open. It was handwritten rather than printed, had no title page, and at the top of the first page I read *Protocol for performing an augury*.

"The instruction manual!" I turned a few more pages. Banking information. The proper storage of *sanguinis sapiens*. "But why do you have it?"

"I asked Lucia if I could bring it to you." Judy folded the tote into a neat rectangle and put it away in her coat's deep pocket. "It's not as if you know any of this."

"No." She'd sounded defensive rather than angry. "And I don't..." Now she sounded subdued. "What you did, with the oracle. I couldn't have done that."

"I'm sure—"

"No. I couldn't have." She let out a deep breath. "All this time, I thought it was just Nathaniel being spiteful, not wanting me to be the custodian. Now I wonder if he didn't know something everyone else didn't. You saved the oracle. It really is what you're meant to do."

I gaped at her, completely at a loss for words. "Judy..."

"Anyway, that's what I think." Judy was suddenly her old brusque self. "Though you really ought to have proper instruction. The manual is useful, but look how big it is. You'll never be able to find anything."

"It'll take time, sure."

"So I thought..." She finally looked directly at me instead of everywhere else in the store. "You could use some help, and I've had all the training. I'm sure the Board won't have any trouble assigning you an... assistant."

Her rosy cheeks were bright red. "You'd want to do that?"

"Why not? I mean, you'd be lost without help."

I smiled. "Come on upstairs," I said. "I think you should see where Silas lived."

ABOUT THE AUTHOR

Melissa McShane is the author of more than twenty fantasy novels, including the novels of Tremontane, the first of which is *Servant of the Crown;* The Extraordinaries series, beginning with *Burning Bright;* and *The Book of Secrets,* first book in The Last Oracle series. She lives in the shelter of the mountains out West with her husband, four children and a niece, and three very needy cats. She wrote reviews and critical essays for many years before turning to fiction, which is much more fun than anyone ought to be allowed to have.

You can visit her at her website **www.melissamcshanewrites.com** for more information on other books and upcoming releases.

For news, new release announcements, and other fun stuff, sign up for Melissa's newsletter **here**.

If you enjoyed this book, please consider leaving a review at your favorite online retailer or on Goodreads.

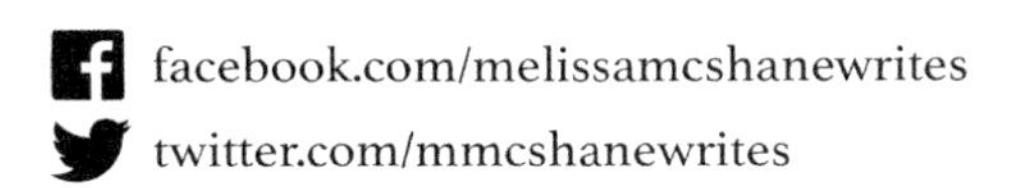

ALSO BY MELISSA MCSHANE

THE CROWN OF TREMONTANE

Servant of the Crown

Rider of the Crown

Exile of the Crown

Agent of the Crown

Voyager of the Crown

THE SAGA OF WILLOW NORTH

Pretender to the Crown

Guardian of the Crown

Champion of the Crown

THE EXTRAORDINARIES

Burning Bright

Wondering Sight

Abounding Might

THE LAST ORACLE

The Book of Secrets

The Book of Peril

The Book of Mayhem

The Book of Lies (forthcoming)

COMPANY OF STRANGERS

Company of Strangers

Stone of Inheritance

Mortal Rites

Shifting Loyalties (forthcoming)

THE CONVERGENCE TRILOGY

The Summoned Mage

The Wandering Mage

The Unconquered Mage

THE BOOKS OF DALANINE

The Smoke-Scented Girl

The God-Touched Man

Emissary

The View from Castle Always

Warts and All: A Fairy Tale Collection

Printed in Great Britain
by Amazon